Where

TOMBOI

Written By
K.K. Thomas

Where Is Love For A?

Written By
K.K.Thomas

Dedication

I dedicate this to the entrepreneurs.

I dedicate Tomboi's who are looking for love.

I dedicate this to the years of building a business.

I dedicate this to those who can not read and that education is hidden from them.

Epilogue

"There is no greater agony than bearing an untold story inside of you"

~Ms. Maya Angelou

Preface

Looking for love while finding yourself in a world that wants to put you in the LGBQTIA

community when mostly you belong to the Black American community can be quite a dilemma.

Growing up, being "in the life" was definitely frowned upon, along with being persecuted for

being apart of the LGBQTIA community by happenstance. My inner complexities make it very

difficult for me to relate to people just on an intimate level. Because, my first commitment is

making sure this world obtains some type of equality from a racial stand point then as a gender

standpoint.

Introduction

This book is a collective of short story scenarios of desired situations with types of women that I would love to fall in love with.

Perhaps in another time, perhaps being a different person.

Falling in love would be a grand desire, I know my eyes show what my heart desires but what my ego will not ask for. Perhaps one day I'll meet her, and she' ll love me and show me how to love. We'll travel the world. Make a mark of love on this universe together. Perhaps we will me in the star. Perhaps we will just be two kindled souls who burn our light separately but some times I still be live there's a her out there for a me.

Table of Contents

TECH SUPPORT

"Hey?"

As she wrapped her head around my office doorway. She was always so cheerful. I can't say I hadn't noticed her. Because, I had noticed, she'd caught my eye. But, I wasn't in the mood to really be scoping any one out.

As I softly smirked, as I seen her face thought, I shake my head and softly smile.

"Um hey, um aren't you like tech support, Web Design?"

"Um aren't you like International Dance? Sike nawhl, yes, I'm something like that, what's up?"

"Well, I need to upload something and it is saying, that the server is not connected or something. Can you come check it out? And no, I'm in neither one of those departments.   But, I'm usually in graphics."

"O ok, that's cool. I guess that is under my job description at times."

"Thanks, you are a life saver."

"I haven't looked at any thing just yet."

"Well, this has to be uploaded by 4am or, yeah, I'll get a strong talking to in the morning, a very strong one."

"Like I said, I haven't seen the problem yet. So don't want to get your hopes up."

"What office are you in?"

We went to a corner office for "Director of Editing", Angel Milagros, was the name plate on the wall.

She pulled out the chair for me to the desk. And, I sat down, took me about twenty minutes, but for some reason her port 1 and port 2 were reconfigured improperly. I helped her upload the files and it was done by 1:50am and backed up and ready for the morning refresh of the home page.

"Señora Milagros, aqui."

"Este senorita."

"Oh ok, let me stop, I have very few Spanish words in my Spanish word bank. But, yes, here, everything is uploaded and good to go. Looks like there was a reconfiguration during an update earlier and your settings weren't adjusted correctly. But everything is good to go now."

"Ok, all I have to do is upload them and I am good."

"No I've uploaded the files. They are on the server and ready for the morning refresh."

"Oh my God you are awesome, do you want to go out for a drink?"

"No, no thanks, I have to have so many hours on the premises. So, I have five or more hours to meet my hours."

"Well, I'm glad that you were here, you were a life saver. Is there anything I could do?"

"Oh, pizza would be love."

"Sure. I'll order a pizza, anything to drink?

"Sure, a peach Arizona iced tea, please."

"Sure."

"I'll be back, going to grab super tech to the rescue, a pizza."

"Oh, super tech to the rescue huh."

"Yes, you just totally just saved my ass."

"Um ok, as I began to walk back to my office."

I went back down to my office and continued to work on some scripting that had engulfed my whole entire brain. About 40 minutes later she came in with a pizza. I really didn't need the distraction but the food was very much needed.

"I'm back!"

"Oh wow, you really went and got a pizza. That's awesome, definitely appreciate the food."

"So super tech to the rescue, what's your name? I hope you like pepperoni, sausage and green peppers."

"Super tech guy to the rescue, oh that's cute. Exactly what I get, minus the peppers, but vegetables are always needed."

"Do you mind if I eat some pizza with you?"

"Nah, it's your pizza."

"No, it's your pizza, you truly was a rescue tonight."

"If you say so, I am pleased that I could help."

"I usually end up not doing too much of nothing, when I'm here. Everything runs pretty smoothly."

"You know to be honest with you, this is my first problem and I have been here for three years."

She had no idea that I designed the system, but she was definitely pumping my ego.

"That's good."

"Why are you here so late?"

I gave a sarcastic stare towards her and the wall.

"What?"

"I think, I told you that I have so many hours, I need to put in on the premises, and I am usually on call any other time."

"So, how many hours?"

"15 hours a month."

"You only have to come to work for 15 hours?"

"And, be on call." As I finished the sentence. As on call, can be quite a commitment but the pay was exceptional, so there was no argument over here.

"Not a bad deal, huh?"

"No, not at all."

She walked over to where the pictures were.

"I see you have pictures of your dog and is that your son?"

"Yes and yes."

"Are you married?"

"Am I married?"

I had a bad date and was not really in to the topic right now.

I just looked at my hand.

"Nawhl, ringless finger. And, had a bad date last night."

"Bad date? What's a bad date for you tech hero."

"Loud and extra extra aggressive and accusatory."

"And, are you ever a bad date tech guy?"

"Who me? Never?..I chuckled out loud, "how could I be a bad date?"

"Tech guy, I kind of think you mean that and you're adding a little chuckle to make it seem, like you may not be a bad date."

"No, I mean it very much, I so mean it. I think I am pretty good company, for the right people. I mean a bad date is in perspective in the two parties involved. I am boring, but I love exploring the world, and like having new experiences. So, I think given the right person, I am a pretty good date, you know."

"Well how about you ask me out on a date?"

"Well I don't really date people at work, it can get awkward, and for some reason you calling me tech guy says a great deal."

"Oh, tech gal, my apologies."

"No problem, Ms. Milagros."

"Well."

"Well what?"

"Are you going to ask me on a date or not?"

"Am, I being pressured to ask you out on a date?"

"I am pressure."

I laughed and replied.

"Oh, ok, Ms. Milagros"

"I do like some aggressiveness and assertiveness, and the fieriness of a Latina woman."

"So, do you like Latinas?"

"How about you put your number down and I'll give you a call off of work premises?"

She took the sticky note pad and wrote her name down and then took it off the sticky pad and placed the number on my chest near my heart.

"I'll be expecting your call later today. You enjoy the rest of your pizza and have a good rest of your night."

"Thank you, you as well."

She walked out and I actually seen when she was leaving the floor of the building. As she passed my office I slightly yelled "hey."

"Yes?"

"Hold up. I'll walk you to your car."

"Oh, thank you."

We walked to the elevator and I pushed the button.

"So how long will you be here?"

"Probably right before any one comes in, so a couple more hours, probably near five or six."

"O ok, well, you make sure you enjoy your night, well your morning."

"Ok, you too."

The elevator opened up and we stepped in, I asked what floor was she on, but she hit the buttons that were on her side of the elevator. B4 was the level she selected. She leaned on the elevator wall and just stared at me. I felt like when in the cartoons the character turns into a piece of meat.

"You're cute. A lil fluffy, but cute." I was offended and turned bashful at the same time.
"Um ok."

"I don't really date women really, but if they're cute I consider dating them. So, what are you a stud or something?"

"No, not at all, although I am often mistaken for one. I really don't get in to labels, but if one needs to know, I guess I'm bi, and a tomboi."

"Oh, bi huh?"

"Don't make me regret walking you to your car."

"I don't think, you're going to regret walking me to the car. You may regret solving my problem tonight."

"And, why is that?

"Because, I don't know, I'm overwhelmed with gratitude towards you."

I had no idea what that meant. But the elevator doors opened and we walked, she clicked her car alarm and the hood popped up and she walked to her trunk.

"Ok."

"Ok, put your number in my phone."

"You left your number upstairs."

"I know, but I want your number."

I took her phone from her hand as she handed it to me, and put my number in it, it vibrated in my pocket and she chuckled.

"Enjoyed that?"

"What?"

"Nothing."

"Ok, have a good night."

I helped her in to her car closed the door and all. Then headed back towards the elevator.

I took the elevator back up and headed to my office. I worked on some things until about five o'clock and the office team came in. They set up like the coffee and put out the breakfast that the office offered, pastries, muffins, bagels, nutra-grain bars, things like that for the office.

I packed up my backpack and finished a few things. One of the older crew members who was familiar with me peeped in and asked "would you like a coffee señorita?"

"No, but if there is any sports drinks, I'll take that, a yellow one please."

"Yes, I will bring it when I come back through." She said, in a heavy Spanish accent.

"Ok. Muchas gracias señora. No problema, muchas de nada.

It was about fifteen minutes when she came back thru "tu bebida."

"Gracias, ma ma."

As she was handing me my drink, a text came through on my phone.

"Come see me, I'll make you breakfast."

I wasn't really talking or seeing any one for someone to offer me breakfast, it was an unexpected text for me. But, it reminded me of Ms. Milagros's number. As I picked it up off the desk and compared it to the number that was texting me.

I texted back after verifying that it was her number.

"I'm actually headed to the gym."

"Well, come get breakfast after the gym."

"Come get breakfast after the gym?"

"Sí, come get breakfast after the gym? And, don't tell me no."

"Um ok."

I'm not going to lie, I like forward women as long as they are caring. Like I don't like loud forceful women, who are mean, or like to use you. I'm pretty sure I have mommy issues. So, I like a very nurturing woman. She was very attractive but she was moving a little bit fast for me. But, you can't be upset at a woman who knows what she wants. It's all about how often she does this and how many people she does this for, or makes feel special. I don't care much if a woman has many friends, it's just a matter of; don't be making other people feel as special as you make me feel.

I finished backing up my back pack and shut down my office lights and headed to the car, and was on my way to the gym.

I got to the gym and it was still pretty empty thank goodness. An empty gym is heaven, you get to work on whatever you want to, today was my arm day and my stretch day. I stretched for about forty minutes, then worked on my arms, then hit the treadmill for a half an hour.

I was selecting my music for the treadmill when a text came through.

"Make sure you text me when you are on your way here. Here is the address."

She definitely lived in the Spanish part of town. That was alright with me, but it let me know that she was still very in tuned with her culture, and I'm not going to lie, I stereotypically wondered if she lived alone. You know with Spanish women they aren't allowed to move out until they are married or something.

I responded back.

> "Sure, I am about to hit the treadmill for an hour and I'll be on my way, I'm in the west side
>> of town, takes me about 30 minutes to get up north."

> "Ok, see you soon."

> "Ok, see you soon." I chuckled, to myself and hit the treadmill.

I definitely was in a ninety's hip hop mood, I put on some "Big Daddy Kane" and ran it out to "Long Live the Kane" album. I got a good run in, I was almost up to running for twenty-five minutes straight, I was aiming to get up to the length of the "Broad Street Run" ten miles, so, I could run that race. Also, I wanted to start having my own running event along the Underground Railroad trail. Twenty-five minutes and the rest of the hour, on and off. I finished out the album and wiped down the machine. I was a bit confused at if I should shower at the gym or not. I really didn't bring extra clothes with me. I usually just left in my work out clothes. I decided to go as I was, since it was such an impromptu link up, I mean what was I supposed to do.

I texted her that I was leaving from the gym and was sweaty. She returns the text.

> "That is alright, I don't mind. I know you weren't really aware that you were coming to see
>> me today. See you soon."

I grabbed my things out of the locker, headed to the car and headed to her house. It took me a little bit of time because morning traffic was a bit congested. I double checked the address and had to loop around the block because her street was a one-way street. I was actually somewhat familiar with the area, I'd drove through the area a bit in my younger days. It took me a minute to find a parking spot, but one car was pulling out across the street from her house, after I circled around, one had cleared.

I texted her and asked was it alright for me to park there in the spot that was clearing out, she said it would be fine. I parked and then I see the door open to her house. I closed the door to my car and clicked the alarm, I squeezed past her car which was parked in front of her house. About time I got to the door she was sitting on the sofa.

"Close the door behind you."

I closed the door, I stood there, I was never one who sat down without being offered to sit down, she told me to come sit next to her.

I sniffed and I said, "I do NOT! smell breakfast."

"I wasn't certain as to what you wanted."

"So, there's no breakfast?"

"There's breakfast, I just wanted it to be hot for you, I wasn't sure what you wanted."

"But, I thought you were making me breakfast."

"I am, do you want eggs, bacon and grits or, what do you want for breakfast?"

"I don't know, I am not really good with options. I mean some sausage and home fries would be good."

"Ok, so I'll make eggs, sausage and home fries. Did you want to take a shower?"

"A shower?"

"Yes, you just came from the gym?"

I looked quizzical.

"Ok, how about, I want you to take a shower."

I looked still perplexed towards her.

"And, what do you propose that I put on?"

"I'll go to the store and get you a tee and some shorts."

"Um ok." I replied.

She went upstairs and I heard a door open. I looked around, her place was very nice and clean. Stereotypically I thought, the Spanish aspect again.

She came back down the stairs.

"Do you live alone?"

"Yes, why?"

"I just asked, because I am about to take a shower, I wouldn't want to burn any one's eyes."

"Si, viva sola, but my family basically owns the block, my momma lives across the street,

in front of the house you parked in front of, my cousins and aunts and uncles live

throughout   the block."

"Oh ok."

"I laid a wash cloth and a towel out for you. I am going to go to the store and get you a tee

and some shorts."

"Um ok."

She left out the door, I sat there for a moment, I can't say I don't end up in these situations but the female is never aggressive enough for any thing to happen. And, I'm very shy and respectful so, I never make a move. So, nothing usually happens. I was a bit stuck and perplexed and really wondering what was with me that I was there. I waited about five minutes and headed to the shower. It took me a minute to figure out how to turn on the shower on, she'd put out a bar of soap, I really wasn't familiar with the brand of soap, it was a bit feminine and really wasn't something I would buy. But at least, I thought, that not too many male or masculine energy people were around since she had this type soap. But, as I thought, it was very convenient that she had a plan to go get me clothes from the corner papi store. I heard the door close and I heard the bag as she walked up the steps. She knocked on the door.

"Hey, here is your shorts and your tee, and I got you a bar of soap, I didn't know if you were going to like my soap."

"Well, I already started using the soap."

She walked in the bathroom and put the bag on the top of the toilet.

"Thank you" as I said.

"Do you want me to turn the heat up for when you get out."

I didn't think much of it, but I responded with.

"You can turn it up a little, that's fine."

"Ok, I'm about to start breakfast, ok?"

"Ok."

I showered for about 15 minutes, I was actually glad she did turn the heat up, because after I wet my hair, I was going to definitely be cold.

I dried my hair and dried off. I grabbed the papi bag and put on the black tank top, tee and shorts she got from the papi store. I headed down stairs. The food smelled good, she'd made some breakfast sausage and some potatoes and she had the eggs sitting there to be cooked, she had some fruit out as well.

"Do you want coffee, tea or juice?"

"I'll take some juice." I responded.

She finished preparing breakfast, then brought it out to the living room where I was waiting. She put the food on like these tray type things wicker type two handles food serving trays, she handed me my tray and then went back to retrieve her tray from the kitchen. I was saying grace over the food, she smiled.

"Amen." She said when I got to the end of the grace prayer.

"Thank you for who prepared it huh?"

"So, you're going to make fun of my grace though."

"No, I thought it was cute and I liked that you said grace."

"Oh, ok."

"So… I think I might be interested in you?"

"You may be interested in me?"

"Yes, you said you weren't seeing anyone right?"

"I think, I said, that I wasn't married."

"If, you were seeing someone, you wouldn't be here?"

"How do you know that?"

"I know, because I can tell what type of person you are and… you would have had to check in by now if you were dealing with someone, who you were really dealing with."

"Um ok."

"Is your food okay?"

"Yes, it is, you can cook pretty good. And thank you for the apple cranberry juice, it is one of my favorites."

She picked the strawberries up and put one to my lips.

"Bite this."

I bit the strawberry and she finished biting it with me. She started kissing me deeply. She rubbed my thighs.

"You're so cute, why are you so shy?"

I know you aren't, as she pulled away from me. She took her robe off and under it, was a lace lingerie two piece, it fit every curve she had, it almost looked as if she had a corset on, her body was very beautiful in the feminine form. She laid me back on the couch and took my hand and put it on her thigh butt area.

"Touch me."

She began kissing me, "Tommie!"

"How'd you know my name? I chuckled.

"You think, I would invite you over and not figure out your name. The lady who gave you t the green Gatorade is mi tia."

I chuckled, "oh ok." \

I felt a little more comfortable with her and began kissing her back.

She said, "Si papi besime dura." She began grinding in to me and grabbed my breast.

"You feel so strong, I like how you feel papi."

I was definitely turned on. I was a little more into it, then when it all began. I wished we'd done this on an empty stomach. But I was going to go with the flow. She put my hands between her legs

"Touch me papi."

I began massaging her vagina lips, she was saying.

"Si. Si papi, gracias papi, you feel so good."

She pulled down my shorts and put her warm vagina on mine and began grinding in to me, she was using me using my body to enjoy her self.

"Papi you feel so good."

I began grinding back in a stroking manner.

"Yes papi" I grabbed her hips and grind-ed deep inside her.

"Yes papi tócame, siénteme, haze llegar papi, sí."

I took off the top of her lingerie and engulfed her breast she had big nipples that got hard in my mouth as soon as I put them in my mouth.

"Sí papi, gracias papi, gracias. Me gusta, me gusta tu boca en mi, si."

… she put her hands in between my legs.

"Si eres dura, eres dura, si." She was was rubbing my clit so good I whispered

"fuck, fuck mami yes."

I whispered "don't stop."

She replied "I'm not papi."

I was firmly squeezing her breast and sucking and licking her nipples and squeezing her breast, she started grinding hard. I figured she was about to come.

"Puedo poner mi cono en tu boca papi?"

"Que ma ma?"

"Can I put my pussy in your mouth?

"Yes mami, yes, put it in my mouth." I replied.

She stood up on the sofa and climbed up to my mouth and placed her pussy in my mouth and slowly softly grinding my mouth.

"Papi I'm coming , I'm coming papi." And she came, she slid down in-between my legs.

"Papi, eres mucho dura, eres dura for mi papi?"

"Si mami!"

She put me in her mouth and sucked me slow and sloppy. I ran my hands through her curly long hair and gripped it and guided her mouth to my climax.

"Fuck mami, you feel good."

"Papi you taste good."

"Fuck!"

As I quivered into an orgasm. She climbed up and laid on my chest and in my arms kinda.

"Papi you feel good. I like that."

I kissed her forehead, I hadn't had an orgasm in a very long time and she got me there. She began kissing me.

"Papi you feel so good."

I am not sure why she kept saying that, but I reckon she enjoyed her self. She laid in my arms. We fell asleep for about two hours. She got up and asked me did I want lunch.

I told her "I'm okay there is still breakfast food there."

She said that she would make me lunch, I told her it was probably time for me to go.

"But I want you to stay."

"You want me to stay?"

"Yes. I want you to stay."

"Mamí, I don't even have clothes."

"Well go get clothes and come back. Tommie, I like you. And it's not just physical, I would really like to get to know you."

"You just had your mouth on me, I think you know me pretty well."

She pout pouted and put her hand in-between my legs and replied

"I want to really get to know her."

I had to pull away from her hand because my clitoris was going to begin to get erect again.

"Mmm she likes me, doesn't she?"

She put her breast on my lips.

"Don't be shy, the girls like you too. Look at them responding to you."

"Mami let me go home and get my bearings right and I'll give you a call."

"You promise."

"Yes. I promise."

"Ok papi. Call me. Did you want to take a shower before you left?"

"No, I'll take one when I get home."

"Well at least wash your face or you can just leave me on your face. I'd like that."

"Ok mami."

"I'm going to cook you dinner tonite ok."

"Mami."

"Yes papi."

"Ok, I'll be back for dinner."

"Ok, that's a deal." she said. She let me get dressed.

"So, you'll leave the other tee and shorts here ok."

"Ok Mami."

She kissed me and walked me to the door and kissed me again.

When I left, her mother was at the door telling her that she needed her to do something. They were speaking in Spanish, and although I knew some Spanish I needed people to speak slowly for me to understand. Her mother spoke to me, I responded with.

"Señora, buenos tardes."

She said.

"See you later." to me and smiled.

I think she liked I was respectful to her mother. I got in the car and shortly pulled out the spot.

LITERAL'S TOY

"Come here literal. Come here boy."

I walked over to hear my dog pouting. Another dog having his chew toy. I reached down to get the chew toy out the dog's mouth, as I hear.

"Merci!"

Pronounced like part of the French phrase thank you. Being said in a calling manner. I see the dog respond a bit but prefers the chew toy.

"Sit, literal sit."

Literal lays on the ground wanting his chew toy but being a good boy.

"Merci!"

I pick the dog up high and ask.

"By any chance is this Merci" said trying a French accent but coming out very black American south northern east coast.

"Oui Merci beaucoup, Thank you, pardon." She said with a French accent.

"You're welcome no worries."

I hand her the dog and separate the dog from the toy in the process. She puts the dog on the ground and leashes her. The dog starts to whimper as I gave the toy back to Literal. Literal began chewing the toy. And looked at the dog whimpering. Merci continued to whimper we began to walk our separate ways.

"Pardon. Do you know where I can get something good to eat around here. Preferably sirloin."

"Um sure." Her English was very good. But I was still trying to think in the little bit of French that I knew.

I asked "do you speak English."

"Oui, I mean yes. I am American" as she still said with a French accent. "I grew up in France."

"O ok."

"Yes, I am very accustomed to American English. You are fine." She giggled.

"Um ok. Well, sure you go…"

She pardons herself and says with her accent.

"Well technically. I imagine they do not allow pets, no?"

"Well, I'm not certain, I think that some people tie their pets on the curb. But some of the restaurants are pet friendly. But now that you mentioned it. The direction I was pointing you I have never seen pets near this location."

"Ok, well may I give you my number and you text me the information. I could not leave Merci outside. Le collar is too big and she keeps slipping out of it."

"Oh ok."

Just then, Literal dropped the chew toy in front of Merci. For Merci to have.

"Aww hoooow niiiiiice." She says "he is sharing with Merci. He is kind. You must be kind too, the owner."

"I guess." As I responded.

"Well thank you and I hope that you and…"

"Literal" as I filled in the pause.

"Literal have a good evening. I am Status and your name."

"Davi."

"Oh well, it has been nice to meet you Davi. Well you two enjoy your evening. And please do not forget to text me the informacion."

Her French accent was crazy…

We waved and I told Literal to say bye to Merci.

I leashed Literal and we walked to the car.

"Literal did you hear their accents boy. They were cute."

He whimpered to comply.

"Wow. Anyways … food and a shower boy."

He barks and sticks his head out of the window. To start catching the wind. As I pull off.

I pull out the parking spot and we head to the house. We get home and clean up the yard. I feed

literal. I hop in the shower. And, when I got out I had received a missed text.

"Davi, this is Status if you could text me the restaurant information, I would like to have

them deliver me some sirloin, please."

"Hey here's that information that you wanted on the restaurant." As I texted back.

"Thank you."

"No worries, enjoy. I hope it is to your liking."

"I am pretty certain it will, if coming from your recommandation." Said with a French accent.

"Thank you, but, I cannot say my recommendations are always what people want."

She chuckled. "Thank you."

"Your're welcome. Enjoy."

I finished up some paper work and worked out, I received a text. It was nine fifty pm and wasn't

expecting any texts.

"Davii are you busy?"

It was Status.

"No, I am not."

"Merci and I wanted to know if you and Literal wanted to go for a walk, are you close by to

center city?"

"I am about ten minutes away and sure Literal and I want to go for a walk. Give me thirty minutes, where are you?"

"We are at the Hilton down town"

"Ok."

I put Literal's good black collar on him and I put on some Shy Designs shorts and tee on. I was glad I had just worked out my muscles were still a little cocky. Literal and I hopped in the car and headed down town. I was in Delco, so I wasn't that far away from down town. Traffic was sweet, so, we got there in eighteen minutes exactly.

She was down in about two minutes after we arrived. She came down and the valet opened the door for her and the little fur ball, Chow Pomeranian mix type of dog. She bent down and picked the pup up and got in the car, as Literal went to the back seat. "Merci" as she thanked and tipped the valet a twenty. He tipped his hat graciously and closed the door.

"Where did you want to go for a walk."

"Bonsoir." she kissed me on the jaw line.

"Oh, um hello."

"You can pick the location." Her French accent being heavily present.

She buckles her seat belt and we pulled out of the hotel parking lot. We went right over to West River Drive. It was a beautiful night and the air was warm with a slight crisp. She had on some shorts with a hoodie definitely from the female's section of the store, it wasn't a bulky hoodie a thin hoodie with a very open neck line.

Took us about 5 minutes to get to West River Drive and park near Boat House Row. We leashed the mutts and started to walk. I pointed out how far the entire walk was in distance and for her to let me know when she wanted to stop walking. She said "ok" and chuckled and grabbed my arm. At the elbow threading her arm to meet at her elbow.

"So, Davi what is it that you do?" Something prompted me to ask what was funny.

"Um nothing. I am crême Philadelphia. Ya mean. That jawn over there is Boat House Row where the row team be keepin' they boats."

She let her French accent go. And, I chuckled as it was still present but she proved her point.

"What do I do? I am in IT love. And yourself?"

"I am in fashion and fabrics, textiles and materials."

"Ok, so, if you are from Philadelphia why do you have a French accent?"

"I left when I was 13. I was offered a contract and I went to France."

"Oh, so you are a model?"

"No, la modélisation was not for me" as she said with a very heavy accent.

"I could not tolerate being confined to such schedules. For so many reasons, fashion, business, print, there were so many deadlines. But, what I did know was fabrics. So, the design side is where I belonged. I go around the world getting the best fabrics for the designers. And, since my father's from South Philadelphia and in to concrete and materials. I was very knowledgeable in that industry and decided to capitalize in a similar industry. About sixty three percent of the concrete and marble that comes in to Philadelphia I am for importing to Philadelphia."

I actually found all of that to be impressive.

"I don't come home often. And, the city has changed so much since I was 13. This is why I needed your recommendation on the restaurant."

"Ok, that's pretty impressive" I replied.

"Is there a dog park near, where we can unleash the dogs and sit and talk?

It was near ten forty-five, I had no specific place to be, and deadlines and I weren't the best of friends either. Although, taken seriously with other people's time and money, but, I did not take on things that I needed to rush to complete.

There was a small park down the street, it was little walk. We walked and talked and then sat once we arrived at the park and unleashed the dogs.

"So, IT huh."

"Yes, nothing major or extravagant as you, but! One of the top IT firms in Philadelphia. Supplying 200 jobs in the urban sector and major contract with the urban re development technology network."

She chuckled and then said "you are adorable." She grazed my face and chin. Are you currently dating? …Wait a minute! So, you do databases and web development."

I chuckled. "Yes. I do. That is majorly what I do along with physical infrastructure and lay out."

"Wow, I actually have two projects in mind. Do you do consultation."

"Yes, I do."

"I actually have a web designer, I just want a second opinion."

"Sure definitely."

"I actually have the papers here with me."

"You have them with you now?"

"No, not on my person, silly. Here in Philadelphia. I go to see him, what's today Monday? I am in the states until Thursday. Next Tuesday, I am to see the web designer. He is charging about two hundred and seventy thousand euro, to build a major site with a data base and shipping infrastructure and shopping area."

"O ok, that is a pretty penny in dollars, is it not? Yes, it is and this is why I would like your consultation."

"Sure, I will take a look at the projects schematics."

"Thanks, and how much do you cost? Your consultation that is…"

There was an awkward mental pause, I had not taking her initial statement any way, until she clarified it with that "that is."

She looked at the dogs and said.

"They get along well, don't they."

They were rough housing but playing.

"Yeah."

"Well it's a little walk, I imagine we should head back to the automobile."

I chuckled.

"Um you're home, you mean car."

She chuckled and said "car" still with a French accent. We walked back to the car. Still conversing on life and the difference around the world and the fact that I should really get to traveling and that my services could be used in so many parts of the world, she was very encouraging without even realizing it.

She was light brown skin with hair down to her shoulder blades it was crinkly you could tell that she was mixed or Latina or Indian or something. She had a tight little body, medium female height, slim. We headed back to the car. I opened the car door for the three of them Literal, Merci and Status.

I Walked to the other side and got in the car. I got in the car and headed back to the hotel.

"Are you busy? I really don't feel like being alone. Would you mind being company tonight."

I always had things to do. But, nothing I couldn't do remotely.

"Let me just check with my scheduler."

I called in to my scheduler. And asked what was on my schedule for the next day or two. I was clear and good to go nothing for the next couple of days that needed my immediate attention or personal attention.

We arrived back to the hotel and she was really high up in the hotel. Crazy scene at the top. But she then asked did I drink. I told her not really.

"But a glass of wine would be nice."

I told her I recently just got interested in to the wine circa. And, maybe she could recommend a good wine. She explained that she liked red wine and that I should try Petrus Red Bordeaux, if I could ever get my hands on a bottle.

"Do you smoke marijuana?"

I chuckled and said.

"Yes, I do."

"Oh, could you get some."

"I could."

"Could you please."

She wanted a quarter oz. I called my guy told him to come to the hotel he said twenty minutes. And we proceeded to have a conversation. I asked her her heritage.

"My father is Italian and my mother is Native American and Black American."

"O ok that is why your eyes are gray."

"Yes" she replied.

We chatted for a few more minutes when my boy hit me back on the cell phone through text and said that he was like three minutes away. I told him to meet me in the store. I needed to get Dutches. We met in the store did our exchange.

He said "we at the studio tonite ,you in?" Told him "nah, I'll catch up later."

Got back up to the room and Literal is sitting in Status', lap getting all types of loving. Merci just chewing on the chew toy that was Literal's. I chuckled.

"Davi, I am in town for a couple days, do you mind keeping me company?"

Um I'd never been asked such a question. My boy hit me back and asked was I sure about the studio. Status asked why my demeanor changed, I explained to her that I was asked to come to the studio

"Aww must you go?" She responded.

"No that is my friends they are in the recording studio and asked did I want to sit in."

"A recording studio. Oh, I want to record."

"You want to record?"

"I always loved to sing." She said.

"Well whenever you want to go to the studio, we can go to the studio."

"Let's go now."

"Now?"

"Now."

"Ok…. the dogs will be alright …Literals a good boy isn't he." As she rubbed her nose against Literal's.

And I looked at Literal and Literal looked at me as to say don't be mad I'm getting my kisses.

"Um ok."

"Is the studio far?"

"No, it isn't far."

Actually, the studio was just finished and she was going to be the first to test it out. I'd purchased the old Amoroso building and the adjacent buildings and two more in the immediate area. She asked could she shower and I said "yes." She showered quickly and happily. She was ready soon. She grabbed her small clutch and her hotel key and said that she was ready.

We waited down stairs for the car to come up.

She said "I am so excited Davi, I've always wanted to record and for some reason I feel like

you, I don't know let's go …"

The car came up, I opened her door and tipped the valet after he passed the keys to me.

We drove about twenty-five minutes and it was like a good close to two in the morning.

"I have a meeting in two days."

"I'm not taking up too much of your time am I? These contractors need to bid for our

concrete. That is all I am here for, it is shipped directly here to Europe. And, they are coming up a

little short but they have been coming around. I am here or eight days to go to three meetings. I

don't have much else to do. Being home is a blessing to me. I am rarely here. And, my child hood

friends, not all of their roads are similar to mine.

She indulged in to her back ground. A bit. She was a product of an interracial relationship

the father's family did not completely condone. The father's mother was upset and felt she'd done

something as an Italian mother for him not to marry an Italian woman. When he told her that he'd

just fallen in love with his child's mother. They loved and welcomed her, it was the father and the

father's mother's relationship that was strained.

They were also one of the biggest material companies in Philadelphia. Dating back to the old

Italian days. Hence her dropping twenties to the valet every time she went out. I was impressed

again. As we pulled up to the building and I touched the key pad and pulled up to the side door.

We got out of the car and walked up to the building. I unlocked the studio. She asked was it mine. I

chuckled and said "something like that."

I turned on the runner lights and went to studio 205C. It was my favorite the most

comfortable. Everything still smelled so new. Basically, the studio was built and the files and the

software had been loaded. There were a few things like signage, that needed to be figured out, but

the studio was definitely up and running.

She rolled up and then started talking. Asking how the studio fit in to IT. I told her "in house digital media." She said "Oh, smart, no out sourcing."

"Only if the client absolutely wants it. But yea."

"Do you produce."

"I don't know about produce but I'm great at recording."

I turned on some of the lights and asked her which setting she liked, she chose one and then I cued up some music and turned the mic on. Asked her style of music she said r and b. Threw a couple of beats her way and she found one.

"~The way I am around you… exactly what I need…. my emotions start to control me... wanting your attention and wondering your love… Could you be…. let me know your touch and how you want me to feel... I'm not even going to hold you... I know this is real. Cook your meals and bear your children, staying with you when you're down and out or when you got dem millions.~"

She sang that and it hit nice. She had really felt the beat. We recorded a couple more versus. Added some reverb, ad libs, sound bites and snippets. I eq'd some spots, mastered and finalized it. Let her hear it. She was definitely giddy and happy. She hugged my neck tight and told me she'd always been scared to record and she loved it.

She asked did I sing and could I teach her to record. I told her I didn't sing, but I had a couple of barz. I should her how to create a new track and how to hit the record and pause button.

I found a beat. And went in the booth. Counted down and told her to hit record, when I pointed at her.

"~7seas, so call me an explorer, always with a back pack so call me dora! back pack, back pack, my flask and my dutch, like bikes and a manual clutch, will fuck with an automatic. Chambers or clips, usually my enemies pic, force muthafuckas in a noose, riddle motherfuckuhs like the Riddler and Dr Seuss, one shoe two shoe, bottom shoe red shoe and

no conscious, so dramatic, I'm bonkers. Heavy duty like cat and tonka,~"

She clapped and said.

"That was good. You can really emcee can't you."

"Emcee. I guess."

"Yes emcee."

"You mean rap?" You're home.

"Well you need to stop being so closed minded and no emcee."

I went back in the whisper booth and did another verse and some ad libs.

"Have you ever considered... I cut her off. "No, I haven't. I suck at hooks. Lyrics for

days... hooks not so much."

"O ok that's."

"Did you want to do another one?"

She said "No, I am tired out. Can we head back to the hotel?"

We were walking out of the studio and I see my boy as he was walking down the hall from getting

food.

"Good to see you in the building."

"Email me the song and I'll give it a listen."

"Ok, in your inbox in the morning."

I returned to our conversation as I contemplated the we aspect of what she said.

"Yes, I'll drop you off."

"Oh, you can't stay?"

It was close to six am. I could stay, but situation was just mad weird, but so, be it. Called

my answering service/scheduler let them know my plans. Although I had no plans, I was still a content manager for quite a few accounts. Checked in with them and about the same time arrived back at the hotel.

"Um can I grab a shower?"

Although I hadn't been in these clothes all day, it felt kind of like I was in these clothes all day. She said.

"Sure. I actually have clothes that you can go through, from designers."

They were from the designers and the brands that always sent her some things. She had some Umbro shorts and tee that I grabbed and we chilled and smoked. She started asking me about life and what was I doing with mine. I thought I'd done pretty alright.

And said "well at the end of the day, have a proper burial anything else in life is a blessing, I imagine."

She agreed.

"Davi do you find me attractive?" Her accent begins to thicken.

"Sure, you are very cute."

"You are so adorable."

"Am I pretty, am I beautiful to you?" As her accent stayed strong.

"Yes, very much so."

"I think that you are very sexually enticing without knowing. You know you do not have to sleep in the other room you can sleep in the master bedroom with me."

The adjacent room was the room with the heap of clothes in it, although the sleeping area was clear.

"Come, come, talk with me."

We sat and talked for a while, she laid in my arms.

The shirt was a tad tight. She advised me to take it off, but I wasn't comfortable doing so. We talked she fell asleep in my arms. I was actually wondering why we'd bumped in to one another. But it was nice and I was just going to enjoy the moment.

I eventually took my shirt off, laid on my stomach and went to sleep. Next thing I know I felt something tickling my back. Had to get my bearings because I'd forgotten what the last thirty hours were about. And, that I was in someone else's bed.

I looked over and wondered where Literal was.

Status says.

"I had the bell man take the dogs for a groom, walk and breakfast. I hope that was alright. They should return around 4pm."

"Um what time is it now?"

"It is half past noon."

She chuckles.

"Would like to order breakfast" I waited for you. I am starving but I did not know what to order for you."

"Um sure. French toast, sausage and orange juice is fine. Thanks."

I looked for my shirt. Or the shirt I'd been given. She put it on the chair. As she pointed in the direction of the chair to the shirt. For some reason I felt she wanted me shirtless. And shirtless was not! My most comfortable state in front of other people. At home, fine. She ordered food and then laid back in the bed. I used the restroom and followed suit.

I asked. "Are there any tank tops in the heap of clothes in the room?"

She said. "You're more than welcome to look. But, you're more than welcome to make myself comfortable."

I didn't find a shirt and decided to lay back in the bed on my stomach. I had no clue what I was going to do when the food arrived, but for now, she began to run her finger tips on my back and I began to squirm.

"She chuckles oh your back sensitive I see…"

"Yes." I replied.

She stopped with the finger tips and rubbed my back with her palms. She said that I had a lot of tension in my back. She sat on my back and begin to rub my back. The thing was she had a fucking G- string on. I immediately felt her warm, her moisture on my back. The massage was nice but I was more distracted by what was on my back. There was a knock at the door, it must have been the food.

She said, "Good, I was starving."

She got the door. She must've tipped the bell hop, because I heard him say "thank you." And then she brought the food to the room. She placed the tray on the table next to the bed. As I began to turn over.

She said, "No let me finish your back."

I continued to lay on my stomach and let her remount me, she massaged my back for about ten more minutes and then reached over to the food.

And said, "Now you can turn over. She lifted one leg for me to turn over but not to get up. I turned over and she began feeding me the fruit that was on the cart.

And said, "I'll get up in a minute."

She was feeding me apple slices. When she commented on my breast.

"You have huge breast. They are like huge stress balls. May I?"

I think I was embarrassed, offended and complimented at the same time.

"Do I mind? Do I mind if you?"

"I would like to squeeze them, may I?"

"Um, sure ok."

She began squeezing them and then suggested that the stress in my back is probably due to the weight and size of my breast. I told her that I really never had a problem with them until I go to do something that requires moving fast and then changing direction, like pivoting during basketball. Other than that, I was truly ok with having them. They aren't the best for when you'd like to be an athlete, but I was ok with them.

She said mine "eh, they are ok. They are good for modeling. On a bad day I am a size b cup on a good day I am a small c cup. I thought how obsessed my first girlfriend was with my breast because her breast was small. So, my breast was like her playground. As I shared the story with her…she chuckled.

She said "I see why your ex was obsessed with them."

"O ok …"

We talked about how women are obsessed with body parts like breast and butts.

She squeezed them and then squeezed them together then she put her mouth on them. I was confused and uncertain as to what was going on, but the dogs were gone til four and I told her I was going to spend the few days with her. So, I imagine this is what she meant.

"Davi." as I was enjoying her mouth, I needed to clear my throat to respond. A jacked up yes? Came out.

"I want you to make me orgasm."

"Pardon."

She started grinding her hips in to mine.

"I need you to make me orgasm."

"Um ok."

She had on a G-string with a cut off very high tee, exposing what must have been c's at the moment that said "Babylon."

"Yes?"

"Yes. Ok."

I wrapped her arm around her waist and ran my hand up her shirt to feel her harden nipples, I squeezed them firmly, yet soft.

She said, "Yes."

And continued to ride good.

"Davi. Have me."

"Ok, Yes I will."

I kissed her stomach and removed her shirt and snapped the G-string where it popped off. She was getting frisky and the arousal was definitely setting in, on my side. I turned her over. And put her on her back. I kissed her neck sucking it softly awhile rubbing my hands on her body. On her thighs on her legs, her arms. I went down to her waist and kissed her waist she squirmed knowing that I was about to embark on her woman hood. Her back arched as I slid down a few inches to her triangle.

Softly biting the front of her vagina, slipping my tongue in to her, to tease her.

"I would love for you to taste me. But I want you inside of me more." She said.

Which made me want to eat her even more. She put her leg over my shoulder which gave me a better access to her.

"Davi?"

"Yes?"

"I want you inside of me."

"Yes?"

"Ok."

I slid my fingers in side of her.

"No, no. I want you inside of me. Do you mind?"

I was lost confused and questioning the situation. She knew I was a female. My insecurities began to kick in.

"Can you look in the drawer. I leaned over to the drawer and there was a new strap. She dressed me and begged me to be inside of her.

I asked, "condom?"

She said, "no."

I grabbed my new dyck firmly to put inside of her, holding the top middle part with my hand and slowly and carefully pushed myself in to her. She gasped and dug her nails in to my back. I slid deep back and all the way to let her know I was going to go deep. She arched her back.

And said, "yeessss."

I begin stroking her. As she begins to move with my rhythm. She was enjoying me and her enjoying me made me enjoy her. She spread her legs up, she was quite flexible. Giving me full access to open her up. I caught a good rhythm and made her buss all on the tip of my strap. She grabbed me tight and said "yes." She asked, "can I get on my knees?"

"I want to taste you."

I was with it, but really wanted my French toast.

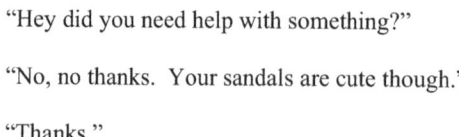

LEAVE YOUR NUMBER

"Hey did you need help with something?"

"No, no thanks. Your sandals are cute though."

"Thanks."

As I was walking in with Breenah's equipment bag.

Cousin was walking out.

"Hey."

"Hey."

We continued walking in our separate ways.

"Dag… what took you so long?"

"Whatever, come on."

I grabbed her hand and led her to the elevator. I pressed the button to call the elevator down.
Breenah had pressed me against the wall, she was asking me.

"What do you want me to tattoo on you?"

The elevator came, Breenah and I got in to the elevator. When we stepped into the elevator, I
selected my floor, and we were standing there.

"Kiss me she" says.

I give a half smile,

"Kiss you, huh?"

She shakes her head in a up and down yes motion and bites her nail tip. I backed her up to the wall,
kissed her, no hands. The elevator reached my floor and stopped. We gazing-ly finished the kiss and
she wiped my lips. I walked out, she followed and we headed to my place.

We walked through the hallway until we reached my door, I pressed the sensor and opened the door.

"Oh, that's neat."

"Thanks, I designed it."

"You can set up right there, is there anything you need?"

"I think I was going with my leaves and my lion, panther and tiger.

"Ok, so am I spending the night?"

"Well I guess, if it's going to take you a minute to do."

"Ok, I'm going to go wash my hands. Can you wipe the table down please?"

She went to the bathroom and washed her hands, I wiped the table down with a detergent bleach type solution she'd put out for me to use to wipe down the area where she was going to do the tattoo.

"Breenah did you want something to eat? I think I was going to order a salad."

"Sure, I'll take one."

"Sure thing."

Breenah set up her tattoo equipment. She tatted me for a while, delivery came, we ate. Then she continued, and we discussed a few topics, religion, money, politics 'til until about two, then I tapped out, it was about four hours.

We fell asleep, on the couch. We woke up about four thirty, and went to the bedroom.

"Pak, you should take a shower."

"Ok. I'm wit' it, that's not a problem."

I hopped in the shower for about fifteen minutes, when I came out, she headed to the bathroom to the shower.

"Have that thang close when I get out."

"I ain't got no problem with that."

"Good."

She spent about 20 minutes in the shower, when she came out she had on a tan teddy made out of silk and lace. She looked sexy as all hail. Just so happened. I went into a tattoo parlor about a month ago, but they didn't have an available tattooist specializing in sceneries, on premises. But I could leave my number. She hit me up, we did a consultation and we've been semi flirting ever since.

She walked to the bed. I pulled back the covers for her to get in the bed. She slipped off her slippers and got in the bed.

"Pak?"

"Yes Breenah? she sat on her knees perpendicular to me

"How many women been in your bed?"

"That's the type of question you're going to ask at this moment?"

"Yes, I want to know."

"Well, if we get past this moment, three."

"Oh ok." She straddled me as she mounted me, she bumped my arm, the arm she'd been working on.

"Sssssss"

"Im sorry baby."

"Pak."

As she leaned down and put her hand over the wrap and kissed her hand as to kiss my healing self-inflicted wound of getting a tattoo.

"Yes?"

"Are you single?"

"You ask questions at very interesting times."

"Yes, Breenah, I am single."

"Ok, good."

"Ok good."

She took my hands and put them on her ass, she leaned down and kissed me. She kissed me and held my wrist firmly, she started grinding on me. I was quickly, very quickly becoming aroused, she had my wrist tight. She kissed my neck and fingers on my inner arms, with her finger tips cuffing my breast and held them firmly. Kind of like a massage it felt nice. It felt good. My arms found their way to the small of her back letting her hips guide the rhythm, I was getting so warm

"Pak."

"Yes."

See, I want to taste you, she slid her lower body into a straight position and then slid down to below my waist, she opened my legs, I looked like a frog on its back, she opened my vagina lips and rubbed the side of my clit with her finger but her nails were long and was actually clinking against my clit heightening my arousal.

"Sssshhh" as I whispered out, I whispered out another sigh. I felt her mouth make contact with my ready to be pollenated flower.

She moaned, "you're jumping all over the place in my mouth, you're getting so hard." Her tongue solidly connected with my clit. Hard, I was damn near close to climaxing, but I didn't want to orgasm yet, because lord knows I was going to need a twenty minute nap,

"Stop baby, I don't want to bust yet."

"But you taste so fucking good, she continued. I'll get it back up."

Fuck she was giving me head so fucking good. I decided to just enjoy it for a little while longer, but I had to get up or I was going to be no good.

I slid from underneath her and flipped her. I laid her on her stomach, put her in the mountain climber position put my fingers in her pussy why she turned on like a faucet. She was grinding my fingers so hard.

"Pak, you feel so good inside me... Pak."

She was grinding her ass in to my crotch so intensely, she was looking for her orgasm and she wanted me to help her find a hard orgasm. She needed me to find it. And, I was going to do just that, I turned her over to her back placed her leg over my should, put her into a sexual Full Nelson and devoured her pussy. I liked her pussy, I kissed her pussy, I sucked her pussy, I savored her pussy, until I sent her legs shaking. She clinched and climaxed.

"Fuck Pak, I'm fucking coming."

"Come baby!"

I came up, kissed her and asked, "can I go deep."

She said a very breathy "yesss."

I reached and got my strapped and got on my knees, she clicked my strap belt in to place.

She said, "let me make it wet."

She engulfed my strap, she was twisting my man-made cock that I was very connected to. I started squeezing my breast and nipples. I turned her back on her stomach and deeply penetrated her, she gasped and told me to pound it, I did just that, got that ass slapping against my thighs until she climaxed again. She screamed, "oh fuck!" She came. She wanted to make me cum.

I told her, "if you suck on my titties and rubbed my clit, I'll definitely cum.

She started rubbing my pussy softly rubbed the clit and grabbed my tits and pinched my nipples, before she put them in to her mouth.

She made me come after we were at it for some minutes and then, I guess we slightly tired one another out, we both fell asleep. Next thing I knew, my phone was receiving an email. It was close to ten, she needed to be at the parlor by 1 to do a tattoo. I checked my inbox, it was my district manager, and she needed a meeting with me. I Responded and she responded back with tomorrow at two, I confirmed and proceeded to wake Breenah.

"Breenah, Breenah, what time do you want me to wake you shawtie?"

"Nine thirty."

"Ok, well, it's ten o'clock.

"Ten o'clock."

"Yes, ten twenty, to be exact."

"Shit, I have a client at eleven thirty. You knocked me out babe."

"Oh, I thought you had a one o'clock appointment."

"I do, but I have a consultation at eleven thirty."

Oh yeah, well its ten twenty onnne twwwo."

As I watch the digital clock turn from twenty-one to twenty-two.

"Pak, can I use your shower?"

"Nah its broke."

"Stop playing" as she threw the teddy she had on last night at me.

Cool souvenir, I smelled it, then balled it up and placed it under my head like a pillow. She walked in to the bathroom, she had a banging ass body, I always wondered how some females tend to their body, I was always on the chubby side, but it helped with not looking too masculine, so it balanced out well with things.

"I yelled through the room, I hope it isn't the type of consultation we ended up having?"

"Never."

"Don't gas me"

She was in the bathroom. I decided to make her an omelette while she was getting cleaned up.

"I'll be in the kitchen, ok."

"Alright."

She came into the kitchen as I was removing then omelette from the pan.

"Hey, made you breakfast."

"Oh, my goodness, you're so sweet."

"I guess, I was just hungry."

"Can you wrap it for me."

"Sure."

"Did you want toast or in a tortilla shell"

"Some toast and if you have jelly."

"Strawberry."

"Yummies."

I chuckled and finish packing up her breakfast.

"Thank you, Pak."

"No problem."

We walked to the elevator, when I pushed the doors, the door opened immediately. The elevator car was already sitting at the floor. We got on and headed down stairs, we walked out of the elevator and through the doors. So, don't go messing that up, "I'll see you at eight thirty."

"Yes."

"Ok."

We reached her car in the parking lot she selected the unlock button from her key chain. I opened the handle.

"Have a good day and I hope you come up with dope designs."

"What your girlfriend around or something?"

"What are you talking about?"

"Can I have a kiss?"

"Well, being as though I have yet to brush my teeth, I figured I wasn't going to try n kiss you."

"Give me a kiss, girl you made me cum like four times and made me breakfast. You gotta kiss a girl if not, she gone think you sending her on her way."

"Well-being as though I don't want a different artist's work in the middle of your ink work, than nawhl I'm not sending you on your way."

"That's the only reason?" She shook her head.

I gave her a very lippy kiss.

"Have a good day Breenah." She started the car as we put the equipment in the car in the back seat, she closed the back door, she got in and I closed her door. She put down the window to the car, I gave her a kiss on the lips.

She pulled off.

I hadn't noticed Markie's cousin pulling in, but I did notice a car pull in about five mins ago. She actually was about twenty paces before me as I adjust my foot in my slides. I walked in and she was at the mail boxes as I needed to go to mine as well.

"Pak?"

"Huh?"

"Have you spoken with my cousin?"

"Cammie, I haven't seen your cousin since we spoke about her birthday."

"Oh shit"

"Yea."

"Ok."

"Ok, well you have a good day."

"Thanks, you too."

I proceeded up, decided to take the stairs, didn't feel like the awkward moment of being in the elevator with Cammie.

I had some time on my hands so decided to head for a run. I showered and brushed my teeth and lotion-ed up, put on some tights, shorts and a hoody and headed to the track. Figured I'd do about a three-mile run. Got in to the zone took about forty-five minutes. I jogged back home, did some core strengthening exercises. Showered again and decided to get some work done.

"Cousin, you don't mess with Shawtie from the building?"

"Oh no, I haven't spoken with Pak in a while. I kinda asked her to be my girl, but the response wasn't there and I was actually talking to someone else."

"O ok."

"Why do you ask?"

"Oh no. Some girl was slobbering her down in the parking lot and you know someone was about to catch a situation.

"Oh nawhl cousin, she good. Aiyte. I may be over later though."

Her cousin laughed, that was code, that she was definitely coming to find out what was up.

"Ok."

Put some time in on some project management bids that my boss wanted me to have for tomorrow. This was a huge opportunity. It was about five p.m. when Breenah called.

"I'm on my way. I need to get you done, the consultation I had wants me to fly out to come two sleeves."

"Ok, that's fine, just don't get sloppy on my shit."

"Now, why would I do you like that?"

"Yea alright."

"Give me a kiss, girl you made me cum like four times and made me breakfast. You gotta
   kiss a girl if not, she gone think you sending her on her way."

"Well-being as though I don't want a different artist's work in the middle of your ink work,
   than nawhl I'm not sending you on your way."

"That's the only reason?" She shook her head.

I gave her a very lippy kiss.

"Have a good day Breenah." She started the car as we put the equipment in the car in the

back seat, she closed the back door, she got in and I closed her door. She put down the window to

the car, I gave her a kiss on the lips.

She pulled off.

I hadn't noticed Markie's cousin pulling in, but I did notice a car pull in about five mins ago.

She actually was about twenty paces before me as I adjust my foot in my slides. I walked in and she

was at the mail boxes as I needed to go to mine as well.

"Pak?"

"Huh?"

"Have you spoken with my cousin?"

"Cammie, I haven't seen your cousin since we spoke about her birthday."

"Oh shit"

"Yea."

"Ok."

"Ok, well you have a good day."

"Thanks, you too."

I proceeded up, decided to take the stairs, didn't feel like the awkward moment of being in the

elevator with Cammie.

I had some time on my hands so decided to head for a run. I showered and brushed my teeth and lotion-ed up, put on some tights, shorts and a hoody and headed to the track. Figured I'd do about a three-mile run. Got in to the zone took about forty-five minutes. I jogged back home, did some core strengthening exercises. Showered again and decided to get some work done.

"Cousin, you don't mess with Shawtie from the building?"

"Oh no, I haven't spoken with Pak in a while. I kinda asked her to be my girl, but the response wasn't there and I was actually talking to someone else."

"O ok."

"Why do you ask?"

"Oh no. Some girl was slobbering her down in the parking lot and you know someone was about to catch a situation.

"Oh nawhl cousin, she good. Aiyte. I may be over later though."

Her cousin laughed, that was code, that she was definitely coming to find out what was up.

"Ok."

Put some time in on some project management bids that my boss wanted me to have for tomorrow. This was a huge opportunity. It was about five p.m. when Breenah called.

"I'm on my way. I need to get you done, the consultation I had wants me to fly out to come two sleeves."

"Ok, that's fine, just don't get sloppy on my shit."

"Now, why would I do you like that?"

"Yea alright."

Breenah arrived in about fifteen minutes. She finished up what she was doing this session in about two and half hours. I couldn't wait for it to heal because this shit was finnuh be leveled up fire. As Breenah was packing up, my door bell rang. I'd just walked in to the bedroom, and when asked,

Pak, do you want me to get that?"

"Sure, I'm not expecting any one."

"Ok."

"Breenah opened the door."

"Hi, is Pak here?"

I heard Markie's voice. I wanted to run to the door, but the thing was, whatever was going to transpire between them was going to happen, the worlds already crashed.

"Babe some one's at the door."

I notice she said babe, but I didn't think too much into it, I waited until Markie called my name.

"Pak"

"Yo", as I came to the door, I knew that there was going to be some type of animosity. But, I just let it go.

Markie asked, "Are you busy?"

I asked if she could give me a minute and that I was going to walk Breenah to the car.

She said "Yea."

"I walked Breenah to the car. I dreaded coming back, she seen her cousin. I knew that was the case and I actually don't know what we had to talk about, there was many loose ends. Yet, I didn't really care to tie them up either. She let it play out the way it plays out and that was that.

"Pak who's that." Breenah asked

"Can we talk about it later?"

"Sure, enjoy your night."

"You too love, be good. Hope u have fun where ever you going."

"Its work not really fun time."

"Hope you do some dope ass work then…"

"Thanks, You be good Pak."

"Yes, Breenah", as I kissed her through the window part of the door.

I walked slowly back up to my spot. When I went in Markie was at the refrigerator. I was a little taken back, to be honest, I was quite over our situation and had moved on. I was a little weirded out that she was in the fridge.

"Um, can I help you?"

"Do you have ice cream."

"Um, no not really, there's some old ice cream in there, not sure if you want that, it's been in there for about four months. "So, I'm not certain if it's still good."

She looked at me as to search for some questions within me, but I wasn't really in to showing any emotions, and wasn't to sure if I had any left for this situation.

She looked in the fridge, her ice cream and envelope was still in the freezer. She opened and took it out of the freezer and the sell by date was just approaching. What is this attached to it, it was your birthday gift, if I remember correctly. O ok she open the envelope and it was her blank plane tickets. She looked at me.

"Pak, you got me two tickets though."

"Something like that."

"What do you mean something like that."

I'd also gotten the custom luggage and the bag.

So, I responded with,

"Well the other part of the gift is in the closet."

"Oh, Pak. Pak?"

"Yes?"

"Who was that?"

I really didn't feel like responding, nor did I think I needed to, I scrunched my face.

"Nah for real Pak, who is that?"

"I chuckled? Nawhl you don't get to ask me that."

She walked up close to me.

"I don't get to ask you that…"

"So, you don't contact me for five months and I am the wrong one."

"If memory serves me correct, you were quite occupied the last time I seen you."

I knew she didn't see me, and I'd caught her off guard, but I didn't care either.

"Last time you seen me was …"

"In dos loco taco"

As I finished her sentence.

She seemed as tho she scanned her memory and remembered the memory instantly.

"You seen me in dos loco taco, why didn't you say anything.

"What was there to say?"

"You're right, I imagine there was nothing to say."

She looked through the drawer to get a spoon.

"You really are going to eat that ice cream?"

"Would you like for me to go get you some?"

I wasn't even sure why I was asking her did she want me to get her some ice cream. I don't know, if I was hurt or mad or didn't care. I was something though.

"Can we walk?"

"I guess, let me put a bra on."

I walked to the room and she followed behind me. I took my hoodie off to put a bra on, it was quite difficult, because of the tattoo. She assisted me with putting it on, I said, "Thank you", slightly soft spoken but appreciative, she returned with a genuine you're welcome.

"Pak."

"What?"

"What?

"What's up?"

"What's up with what?"

"Are yawl fucking?"

"Are we fucking?"

"Why are you asking me that question?"

"Because I would like to know."

"Why do you want to know?"

"Because I'm wondering why you never answered my question?"

"Do I have to?"

"You know you don't have to, but I would like to know, and would like for you to answer my question."

"Um ok, I guess."

"Pak."

"What Markie"

"To be honest I don't know how to answer that question."

"Are yawl fucking?"

"Are we fucking? I don't know. Did we fuck? Yes. Are we going to fuck? I don't know. Have we fucked? Yes. Do I know if we're going to fuck again, I don't know? How thu fuck am I supposed to know?

"No, you answered my question."

I really didn't feel like none of this conversation. We walked out my place to the elevator, I pushed the going down button.

"Pak, to be honest I just wanted to know, I think I wanted to know if you would lie to me more so, over than actually being all in your business. I just didn't like you answer."

"And, I'm not sure if I liked telling you the answer."

"I can understand that."

"And since when do I lie to you?"

"I didn't say that you did, I just wanted to know would you."

"Why would what I do matter to you?"

"I'm not sure, I was just explaining to you why I asked."

"I guess Markie."

She took my hand as we crossed the parking lot. It didn't matter but I was just confused in the entire moment and it was a lot for me to take in. We walked to the store, she let go of my now sweaty hand and I opened the door for her to walk through the door way. I walked to the refrigerators as she walked to the freezer, I grabbed a sports drink, she was still making her decision when I walked to her, I don't know if I want… as she pondered, she open the freezer and grabbed a pint of ice cream, I told her, "grab me a rocky road."

"Oh, you eat ice cream now."

"Something like that."

My phone alerted a text. "Hey at the airport." Weren't you s'pose to, you should have driven me."

I started to text back.

When Markie asked …" what size do you want, .. you text'n shawtie that just left?

She asked as she noticed me texting?

"Wow you asking a lot of inquisitive questions today, aren't you?"

"I'll take that small one please."

As I continued to text back.

"You didn't ask."

"Well I seen you had company ready to come over."

"Wow company."

As I texted back.

"Pak, Pak c'mon!"

I was smiling when Markie was calling me, I was smiling at the text.

I don't think she took to that too kindly. Her demeanor completely changed.

I really didn't know what to say, nor did I know what she wanted me to say. Just when I started to think about letting my guard down, she displayed exactly why I shouldn't have....and I didn't respond, I just remained quiet.

Breenah texted, "Well can you pick me up from the airport."

"Sure."

"Pak, you ate that bitch pussy?"

"What?"

"Markie you are tripping."

"Pak", as she grabbed the bag from the counter and I gave the cashier my card.

"Yo, you're tripping. You do know…"

As I get mid-stream sentence the cashier finished up the transaction. "Enjoy your day."

"Thank you."

"You do know, I haven't seen you?"

"It doesn't mean I don't have feelings for you Pak."

"Markie you're trippin."

"You ate her pussy, didn't you?"

"Yes, I did. Damn."

"Did you fuck her?"

"Yes, Markie I fucked her, what do you think that I do to women, I am intimate with?

"Fuck you, Pak!"

"She fucked you?"

"You, you're the fuck tripping."

"She fucked you Pak?"

"Whatever you say she did Markie..."

"Pak, she stuck a strap in my pussy?"

"You re pussy? Yo…Any ways…"

She took my hand again as we cross the street. I didn't really know what was happening, like it was really a bit much, I mean I hadn't see her in a minute, nor had she called, not to mention she was with someone else when I seen her last. We walked back to the apartment building and to the elevator. I press the button to call the elevator down.

"Pak. I'm sorry."

As she said her apology the elevator opened.

"Is that why you couldn't be my girl?"

"I met her after I seen you with someone at Dos Los tacos Markie."

"You seen me at Dos Los Tacos?"

"Yes."

We'd gotten on the elevator and we were approaching my door.

"I'm sorry Pak. I just felt like you really didn't know what you wanted and I was really interested in you. And you seem so stuck in these labels and roles."

"Labels and roles, no. I'm not stuck in no labels or roles."

"Ok."

"Pak, can I see something?"

"What?"

She was being weird.

"Can I see something?"

I had no clue what she was talking about, so I said, "sure."

She put her hands down my pants and put her finger in my pussy hole.

"You tight."

"Who was the last one to fuck you?"

"What?"

Something in her instinct must have told her, her.

"Was it me?"

"Baby you got me plane tickets and an exclusive purse for my birthday?"

I looked the other way, but she knew everything I was thinking her hands were still deep in my vagina and that bitch wasn't holding no emotions back. She was being vulnerable as fuck flinching and getting wet.

"Pak, did you miss me?"

I slowly slid her fingers out my pussy and took them out of my pants.

"It don't matter though.

"It does matter."

"Why does it matter."

"Because, I've missed you."

"Look Markie, I have a meeting tomorrow early, I was actually having an early day."

"Can I spend the night?"

"Can you spend the night?"

"Yea, I missed you."

"I guess Markie, let me change my bedding."

She said, "let me help."

"I guess." I changed the sheets, she helped and put them in the hamper.

I headed to the shower. My emotions were lost, I knew I liked her, but, it didn't seem like there was an openings place for us. I knew that I was emotionally broken and wasn't really up for opening up. I was in the shower thinking but not too much. Took a shower came out lotion-ed up. She hopped in the shower, I was catching the rest of the game. She asked for a tank top and got her ice cream.

"Pak."

"Yes Markie?"

"What are you afraid of?"

I'm not afraid of much, I don't know? I guess getting sprayed by a skunk or…"

"No, in a relationship?"

"Why couldn't you be my girl, what was missing"

"Markie. What made you come here?"

"One hundred?"

"One hundred."

"Breenah called me, because she didn't know we'd stopped talking."

So, were you going to call or stop by before that?"

"I don't know. I just know when she told me, I didn't like the feeling I felt at the thought of
you with someone else."

"I guess Markie."

"I guess Pak."

She walked and put the rest of her ice cream back in the freezer.

She came back up and sat on my bed.

"Pak?"

"What Markie?"

"Do to me, what you did to her."

"What?"

"I missed you Pak."

"I was just with another woman Markie."

"Pak... make love to me."

She started kissing my neck and massaging my breast. My nipples became instantly aroused
and alert.

"See you've missed m too?"

Did you miss me Pak? It's ok if you have."

She was feeling nice and yes, I had missed her, but why, why should I give in to her
physically? I had no choice I was becoming so wet, she was just making joke after joke.

"Damn puddles. Singing in the rain. You can't stop the rain. Did you miss me Pak? Can I have some pussy Pak? You kept it tight for me, that shit turns me on Pak, that you haven't let anyone inside of you."

She straddled me and took her top off, her titties expose, calling my mouth and my mouth yearning for them back. She reached in the drawer, and got her strap out the top of the night stand.

"She still here."

She put on the harness, she put some lube and leaned down and said although you don't need it,

She softly asked.

"You gone let me in?"

I heavily whispered.

"What?

She said, "say yes."

She started going inside of me, "say yes."

As she pushed herself inside of me. As I started to say yes with her in the same rhythmic pattern.

"Yes."

"Yes." as we simultaneously said.

"Fuck baby, I've missed you, this pussy still good all day though, it's been waiting for me."

She pulled out.

And, went down, she licked my pussy flat tongue style, the she sucked my clit, then went back in to my pussy with her dick.

"Pak, I'm hard as fuck for you right now."

She started stroking my pussy and, sucking my breast just like I liked it, I started leaking all over her dick.

"Damn baby, you're so wet for me, you're so fucking wet for me?"

She started stroking in an upward motion. She was massaging my pussy so good, I started to feel the tremble. She slapped my legs and said.

"Don't let no one else taste this pussy, she was on her knees directly in front of me stroking my pussy, Pak, I want this pussy."

What she was saying was turning me on, and I felt that she was looking more for verbal queues than physical ones. I think she knew she'd conquered me physically. It was verbally she was trying to defeat me at now. And, I just couldn't bring myself to give in to say the things she wanted me to, although a piece of me wanted me to.

She asked, "Can I have the pussy?"

There was no way that I could say yes, but I did respond with a, "baby you feel good."

And, she did. She was stroking my walls so gawt damn good, she was goin' so deep and slow and firm. She strokes my pussy so good, I came so hard. I'd never cum like that before. She went down and sucked my clit just like I liked it suck. She put my ass right to sleep.

I woke up about a hour and forty five minutes later, and there was no way that I could let her have that win. I topped her as she laid on her stomach and kissed every vertebra downwards and licked my tongue upwards. Once I was finished kissing her spinal-cord, she allowed some soft mfs out, which let me know that she was enjoying my kisses.

"Damn, I've missed you."

I was shocked that she'd said that, but it felt so good. I finished kissing her spinal-cord put her in a kneeling position and begin to rub the petals to her flower. She was the perfect example of a Georgia peach in that very moment. Looking like a perfect spring time treat. I enjoyed her, I enjoyed her body, I enjoyed her emotions, her happiness, her sadness, her fears, her strength.

I prompted her that I wanted her, almost needed her to turn over. She turned over, I didn't mean to turn in to a sixteen-year-old boy and suck her neck and give her hickies while grinding into her pussy. When she was getting so wet it was all over my thighs. She moaned.

"You make me feel so good baby."

That shii stroked my ego real tough.

MY CHOCOLATE ICE CREAM

Standing in line waiting to pay for my ice cream, I hear.

"Chocolate ice cream is boring."

I shake my head "um, I guess" as I turn my head.

"5 E, right?"

I replied with a "yes."

She looked familiar and I recognized her from the building.

And followed up with.

"It's for MY Milkshake."

"Oh, YOUR Milkshake."

"Yes, My milkshake."

"Well, enjoy your milkshake."

As I was next in line and it was my turn "$4.29" as the clerk rang me up.

"Have a good day."

"You too", as I responded to the clerk.

"Have a good day," as she mocked the situation.

"You too, cousin of 5 g."

"Stop hawking me." She responded and smiled.

"Nah, going to go make my milkshake."

"Going to go watch my movies."

As I stepped outside my phone rang. I took the call which led me to still being out side when 5g's cousin came out side.

"See, hawking me."

As I finished up my call and shook my head. I was a little dumbfounded because these situations can either turn in to a good flirting situation or an awkward argument for me. I just kept it to a minimum.

"You mean, talking business?"

"Call it what you want."

As one of the plastic bag handles drops and she drops some cookie dough oreo nugget srawberryshortcake ice cream concoction.

"This is what you wanted me to get?"

As I helped pick up the water and ice cream.

"I don't think my metabolism could handle any of what was in this flavor of ice cream."

"Oh. you're such a gentle boi" as she takes her ice cream out of my hand. I playfully snatch it back and said.

"Perhaps I just found one, I should try it."

She playfully snatches the ice cream from my hand.

"Are you about to go back to the building?"

"Yes.

"I'm headed that way as well."

I thought it to be a little odd because I thought that I'd just seen my neighbor leave.

"That's chill." as I replied.

I grabbed one of the bags she had. And we began walking. As we were walking she just blurts out.

"Name?"

I look and chuckle?

"Name, huh?"

"Yes, name?"

"Pak."

"O, ok. Markie."

"Hi, Markie."

"Hi, Pak."

We were approaching the building and the elevator. I pressed up and we got in the elevator. She got a text and it was her cousin.

The text saying "I'm running late."

I told her, "it's cool, you could wait in my crib."

"Hawker!"

"Fuck it, you can wait in the hallway, the vestibule, the I don't care."

"I'm just playing. Why you so uptight?"

"I don't know shawtie. Do you want to wait or not?

She found some manners with in her.

Saying "yes" as a response.

The elevator came to a stop, we got off the fifth floor. I put my thumb up to my door and unlocked my door.

"Oh, fancy huh?" As she commented on my biometric lock.

"I guess. I was out kicking the ball and didn't feel like bringing keys that is all."

"O, ok. You can have a seat. Is your cousin close or...?"

"She said "like a half hour."

"O ok. Can I hop in the shower?"

"Yeah you good, that's cool."

"You mind if I roll up."

"Nahwl, I don't mind."

I rolled up and started the shower.

I asked "you smoke?"

She said, "No."

So, I just closed the door and yelled,

"The remotes are on the table."

I had spoke to her cousin a time a two, but I still didn't know her. And, I was smoking, so, I'd begin to hope all of my shii was there when I came out of the bathroom. But, didn't think of it too much. I showered. And, put on some shorts and a tee.

When I came out of the shower, she was watching some shii, that I'd never watched, MTV's Challenge and I so wanted to turn to ESPN. But, I went to make my milkshake. With MY chocolate ice cream.

"A chocolate milkshake."

"Yo, what is it, that you have against my chocolate milkshake?"

She came over to the kitchen.

"You should try this."

As she hands me her ice cream to say she needed a spoon. I think.

"Is your cousin almost here because, I cannot tolerate your non manner having ass."

I handed her a spoon.

"Oh really."

She started talking some light trash.

"Ok, well, you have your little chocolate milkshake and I'll just wait for my cousin in the hallway."

I blended my milk shake as I poured a small amount of milk in to the blender. Paused the blender. I cut her off at the door.

"Look, I was just playing but what are you watching over there and you just hounding my chocolate milkshake. You are more than welcomed to stay here until your cousin gets here Markie."

"Thanks Pak, now back to this chocolate milkshake."

I pouted and wondered what it was about this chocolate shake that she wasn't even taking parts in as she opened her double fudge caramel cherry delight Samoan girl scout flavored ice cream.

Her cousin texted and said she was still stuck in traffic and was going to be awhile. I wondered when could I, turned to ESPN. As I picked up the remote and pointed to the tv to motion-ly ask her was she watching what was on the screen.

"My manners" I thought I was company."

"Shawtie, go ahead." I say, "No good deed goes unpunished."

As I reached out to grab my lap top. She grabbed it too.

"Pak, you are going to get on your lap top?"

"Markie. You said you was watching the tv and I just want to sip my shake. And chill."

I got up and walked to the room to get my el. Shaking my head.

"Are you single?" I asked as I lit my el.

"Am I single? Why you want to take me out...?"

I choked on the smoke...

"Hail nawhl, I'm good ..."

"Hail nawhl? as she replied. What is that suppose to mean?"

"Well I figure who ever deal with you, may have their hands full."

"Oh really?"

She looked back at it and said,

"Well you right, but no, I am not seeing any one right now."

I replied with, "makes sense."

I asked "you smoke?"

She said, "No."

So, I just closed the door and yelled,

"The remotes are on the table."

I had spoke to her cousin a time a two, but I still didn't know her. And, I was smoking, so, I'd begin to hope all of my shii was there when I came out of the bathroom. But, didn't think of it too much. I showered. And, put on some shorts and a tee.

When I came out of the shower, she was watching some shii, that I'd never watched, MTV's Challenge and I so wanted to turn to ESPN. But, I went to make my milkshake. With MY chocolate ice cream.

"A chocolate milkshake."

"Yo, what is it, that you have against my chocolate milkshake?"

She came over to the kitchen.

"You should try this."

As she hands me her ice cream to say she needed a spoon. I think.

"Is your cousin almost here because, I cannot tolerate your non manner having ass."

I handed her a spoon.

"Oh really."

She started talking some light trash.

"Ok, well, you have your little chocolate milkshake and I'll just wait for my cousin in the
hallway."

I blended my milk shake as I poured a small amount of milk in to the blender. Paused the blender. I cut her off at the door.

"Look, I was just playing but what are you watching over there and you just hounding my chocolate milkshake. You are more than welcomed to stay here until your cousin gets here Markie."

"Thanks Pak, now back to this chocolate milkshake."

I pouted and wondered what it was about this chocolate shake that she wasn't even taking parts in as she opened her double fudge caramel cherry delight Samoan girl scout flavored ice cream.

Her cousin texted and said she was still stuck in traffic and was going to be awhile. I wondered when could I, turned to ESPN. As I picked up the remote and pointed to the tv to motion-ly ask her was she watching what was on the screen.

"My manners" I thought I was company."

"Shawtie, go ahead." I say, "No good deed goes unpunished."

As I reached out to grab my lap top. She grabbed it too.

"Pak, you are going to get on your lap top?"

"Markie. You said you was watching the tv and I just want to sip my shake. And chill."

I got up and walked to the room to get my el. Shaking my head.

"Are you single?" I asked as I lit my el.

"Am I single? Why you want to take me out…?"

I choked on the smoke…

"Hail nawhl, I'm good …"

"Hail nawhl? as she replied. What is that suppose to mean?"

"Well I figure who ever deal with you, may have their hands full."

"Oh really?"

She looked back at it and said,

"Well you right, but no, I am not seeing any one right now."

I replied with, "makes sense."

She threw her napkin at me...I picked it up off of my lap and said,

"eww...."

She said,

"You're an ass hole."

"Been told that, a time or two."

"So you're not just like some nerd geek?"

"Nawhl, I'm like a nerd geek asshole..."

She went to throw the spoon.

"If you get chunky monkey grape jolly rancher butter pecan on my upholstery we may have a little problem."

She scowled and showed she wasn't the type to be destructive.

"I think, I'm waiting in the hallway."

I grabbed the remote as she picked up her snack things again. I waited til she started walking and beat her to the door.

"Why? Why you so kinda feisty with me for no reason?"

"Pak, I am waiting in the hallway."

"I mean that's fine, if you wait in the hallway. Can I get a hug first tho?"

"A hug?"

"A hug."

She put her arms out with the bag on her wrist to give a corny ass hug.

I hugged her and put a little pelvis in to the hug to try and graze up against her.

"You know you can wait in here."

"I don't wait with assholes."

"Assholes? Who pestered about chocolate milkshakes? How are you calling me an asshole, when all you did was dog my milkshake, my chocolate milk shake?

She said it was different with somewhat of a cute voice.

"Look you can wait in here and let's not be ass holes."

I leaned against the door and completely came out of the hug. She started to walk back to the couch when I noticed noticed that ass. I had noticed before but I'd noticed and it was in my apartment. My lil shawtie, the man in the boat, was woke and was ringing the light tower.

"So, can we watch ESPN?"

"If you try my ice cream."

"haggaandazsorbetcafelatteespressovanillabean."

"I thought we weren't going to be ass holes."

"Ok, I'm sorry, come here."

She swatted at me as I caught her swat. And pulled her in to me. Lifted her chin to raise her lips to mine, I brushed my lips against her lips, feeling the softness and hopefully stimulating her. I lightly licked her lips as they were still closed, I softly semi quickly sucked on the top one then matching the bottom lip with sucking her bottom lip softer and lighter but more hungrily. She stayed with the kiss, so I went in to a full kiss. We fucked got married had kids…lol sike nawhl…. Tho…. Um…lol I went in to the kiss hovering my torso over hers, forcing her to lean back and relax on the chair. Her leg went up in an inviting way, allowing me to lie on top of her. I immediately felt her warmth and wanted it even closer to me. She put her ice cream down. I stopped to put the top on it and told her,

"That it's probably going to melt."

As she then prompted me to put it in the freezer. I looked and ask ,

"Are you serious?

She asked,

"Are you serious about it melting?"

I hopped up and finish putting the top on and tossed it in the freezer. Came back to her and immediately went back for the mouth and my hands went inside the top. I felt her hard nipple on the palm of my hands, my mouth wanted to devour it immediately. Shit drove me fucking wild. Exactly then, she put her hands in my shorts and realized I didn't have any shorts under my shorts on.

"You lucky you just got out the shower or I would call you nasty."

I put her hands further in my shorts and started kissing her good. I let her play inside my pussy for a while she rubbed my walls nice as fuck then I undressed her.

I got on my knees. I put her legs over my shoulders open up her pussy. She was a little hard for me. I smiled she grabbed my hair and pushed my face in to her pussy. I engulfed her clit, her pussy lips, and pussy hole, and slowly sucked back, I engulfed it again allowing the lips and the clit to still be in my mouth. And getting her clit to be left in my mouth. I closed my eyes and slowly and softly sucked on her clit. I wanted her to grind my mouth hard and passionately desperately for satisfaction… "fuck." She started grinding my mouth real good.

"Shit Pak."

As I smayled,

"What Markie?"

"Pak?"

"mmmmm …"

she bust hard as fuck in my mouth.

I, I rubbed my chin up her torso wiping some of her off of me, as I slid my fingers deep into her throbbing pussy, I rubbed her pussy good as fuck. As I sucked on her titties grinding my fingers against her pussy walls and thrusting my hips in to her body, she grabbed hold of me tight and came again with me inside her.... I rubbed her clit at the base of it underneath until she let out another sigh and bust again.

"Damn Pak..."

"mmm yeah..."

"Pak what?"

"Can I finish playing in that box though?"

"Trying to hear you buss too tho."

"Oh, you wanna help me buss huh...?

"Yeah and I want to buss again too."

Her phone went off. She told her cousin

"She left."

... I'm thinking

"how'd I end up between this bitch legs and all I was doing was playing futbol. At the park."

"I mean a lot of females can't handle the position that'll make me buss for certain its' hard on the knees."

"Oh, you want me to eat your pussy?"

"I mean you can suck my clit, like it's the best dick you ever had but, I'm saying. I pushed her head towards my nipple. She started sucking on it. I put her hands back in my shorts and pushed her two fingers inside my pussy. I started rubbing my clit, while she's inside me rubbing me good as fuck and with my other hand, I opened her legs pushed her to a squatting or kneeling position and started finger fucking her pussy. Once in a while I would take my hands out my shorts to suck on her titties, she would moan which made my pussy jump, which made her moan which made my pussy jump. Shit felt good, she felt good as shii, about three minutes in I could barely hold it. She rubbed the right spot, when I rubbed the right spot and sucked at the right time, I swear I almost squeezed the feeling out of her fingers. And, after I bust, she just went ham and fucked me. I started to pant heavy and whine and say

"Fuuuuhkkk Markie." And asked, "why you fuckin' me?"

She said…

"because it so tight…"

I was so shocked and it felt so good at the same time. I had to stop fucking her and grab her tight like a lil biii, I didn't mind, but … I just got the chills and just bussed again. Shit, was definitely type right.

I rubbed my pussy after she pulled out, she rubbed the extra moisture on my clit and kissed me.

"Damn Pak, that was kind of nice, thank you for that."

"Um yeah, I guess you got me up here feeling like a true little bitch."

"Don't worry next time I'll let you strap up if you want. And who knows maybe you'll want me to strap up…"

"I don't know but that shit definitely got my clit right back up, I put my hands back in my shorts and put my finger inside of me deep and rubbed my clit firmly. She said "mmm."

I said.

"Uh ok, an knawhl, that's just me feeling like a lil bitch again."

"Come here tho."

I pulled her to me and made her ride my mouth, her leaning back playing with my nipples she was squeezing them nice and good. And then she leaned forward and I wrapped my arm around her waisted and fucked her until she bussed again …she bussed again.

She chilled for a little while and then she needed to sneak out the building, being as though she told her cousin she had left. When we looked out the window, we seen her car, which meant she was definitely back.

Haven't Seen You In Awhile

As I rolled out of bed, I was dead ass tired yo. Conventions had me drained, but I was definitely glad that I was doing them. Slid on my slides and scooted to the bathroom. Used the bathroom. And then came back to the bed. Laid back down and as I was about to enjoy the softness of my pillow, I noticed I missed a text. I wasn't scheduled for anything for three weeks. Primarily because my manager was on vacation. I swear he better prorate me those weeks. I could make a substantial amount of money during those weeks. They are almost peek weeks, but when is it not a peek week, and I guess we do make enough money.

But as I looked at the phone. I hit the read button, hey are you sleeping? At the top of the text box it read Markie. I looked at the time and the time of the missed text. Ten minutes had gone pass. I figured she'd still be awake. And text back.

"Hey, um not at the moment."

I laid back down, just in case she'd gone back to sleep, we hadn't really spoke much, although I did not mind receiving a text from her, just placed it as a bit odd.

"What are you doing?"

"At the moment, being a bit annoyed because a mosquito bit me on my finger, and yourself?"

"Wondering if you want company, feel like being company?"

I looked at the clock once again 1:49.

"Um nah, I don't mind. It doesn't matter, but you know my cousin still lives in your building."

"Yes, I think I seen her the other day."

"Ok, well, I'll be over in about twenty minutes."

"Um, ok, I was hoping that was truly more like 40 minutes but we were going to see soon." I thought.

I went to go get into the shower and hoped that I was going to get the chance to shower. Which I was able to and actually was about to fuhk up a piece of apple pie, right before there was a knock at the door.

I walked to the door, left my pie in the microwave and answered the door. I opened the door.

"I forgot you had the entry code to the building."

"That was a good thing, because I didn't know to buzz you in or walk down and get you."

"Buzz me in, don't have me waiting."

"Um ok."

"But you have the code anyways."

"Yes, but buzz me in, don't have me waiting."

"Um sure."

I took her hoodie and laid it on the arm of the chair. I had no clue as to what this visit was about. I walked to the microwave to get my pie, like a little kid extra hype. Grabbed a fork and was about to sit down, when she started.

"That's mine, right?"

"Um no, but the refrigerator is right there, knives in the drizawer, have a go at it."

"Ugh."

As she threw a tissue at me, she was reapplying some lip stick, lip glossy gloss stuff. As I picked up the tissue and said,

"Ewwww, and if this would have hit my pie. You know this is disrespectful, as I dropped the   napkin on the table."

"You aren't going to get your company some pie."

"I don't really look at you as company any more, so we are going to go with no."

"I haven't seen you, nor heard from you in two months and you don't think I'm company."

"Um you text me today right?"

"Oh my God, Pak, why is this conversation going like this?"

"Markie I'm just eating my pie, eating my pie."

"And, if you want some apple pie then it is in the refrigerator. If you'd really like me to get you pie, I will get you some pie."

"Yes, please can you get me some pie."

"Sure Markie."

I take a huge bite of apple pie off of my fork. And put my saucer down on the table and walk to the kitchen. I go to the refrigerator and get the pie and the knife and the saucer out, and I yell a little from the kitchen.

"You want a big piece, a small piece?"

She replies with

"A medium slice and vanilla ice cream please."

"Vanilla ice cream? She lucky, I actually had some."

"Ok Markie."

I cut the pie and scooped the ice cream. I asked did she want the pie heated up. She replied with some sarcasm.

"Who eats cold pie with ice cream?"

"Yo, why do you always have a smart mouth? Like, nwahl for real, why tho?"

"No, I am sorry, I guess how is one suppose to know only hot pie goes with ice cream."

"Look, you could have just devoured a pound, how am I to know."

A chuckle and, "yeah whatever."

"And, why aren't you partaking in your favorite ritual?"

"Um, I don't think it is a ritual, but something is usually twisted for certain."

"Um skeerr skeeerrr, lane change, you know its like damn near three o clock right though.

"Yes, I do."

"I'm just asking are you certain of the time?"

"Yes, I am. I hope it wasn't too much of a hassle. Do you have work tomorrow?"

"No, I do not."

"Ok, so you can sit with me and chat and stuff, right?"

"Um, ok sure."

"I mean, did you have plans though?"

"No, not particularly. Just to grab mad sleep."

"Oh, so you want to go to sleep?"

"Would I like to go to sleep?"

"Yes, would you like to go to sleep?"

"Um, you just got here."

"I know, but if you'd like to go back to sleep, we can go to sleep."

It was strange but quite interesting at the same time. And actually, now that she mentioned it I wouldn't mind, sleeping next to her.

But I replied.

"I said no, I am good so what's up with you?"

"Nothing, work, same 'ol, but to keep it real with you. I find myself thinking about you occasionally."

"O, ok."

"No, really though."

"Yeah, your peeps seem cool, and I see your car some times when you come some times."

"Can't say you haven't crossed my mind."

"Oh ok."

"So, I mean I just want to chill with you, is that ok?

"Um, sure that is fine."

"So, what were you about to do though?"

"I'm not sure, what were you doing?"

"I was just up and had the next few days off. Had today off and found myself wanting some company I think."

"Oh ok, well yeah, I was sleeping."

Ok, well let's go to sleep then."

"Let's go to sleep, just like that huh?"

"Yeah. Um ok"

I went to grab the remote to turn the tv off and headed to the bedroom. I reminded her where the bathroom was and then kicked my slides off and laid down. She used the bathroom, and headed towards the bed, she took all her clothes off down to her panties which were thick banned Victoria's Secret underwear. They were a little cute and sporty. I took my shirt off and just had on some ball shorts. She asked for the remote, and then laid next to me in my arms. She felt so comfortable in my arms. It felt so right, I actually drifted right on to sleep. There were a bit of hours that had gone pass when I felt something on my ear, and I actually forgotten that I had company. I felt soft lips on my ear, and next I heard.

"I want some, can I have some?"

I had to get my bearings and had to understand what was going on. I chuckled and said.

"Good morning."

I kissed her lips... and said.

"You want some of what?

"Pak, I want some of you."

"You want some of me what?"

"I want some of your sex, can I kiss you?"

"Can you kiss me?"

"Um why do you ask?"

"Why not just kiss me?"

"You right."

And she kissed me.

"Pak, can I have some?"

"Markie baby."

I don't know, perhaps I never really seen her in to me or being physically attracted to me. She could have used me as her personal jungle gym, romper room if she wanted or needed to, she ain't have to ask for any permissions, well a few, but not many.

She kissed me and then as she was kissing me started to take my ball shorts off. She managed to get them off and then she straddled me and sat on top of me and started grinding, slow and seductively trying to find our rhythm. That shit got good quick, she bent down and started nibbling on my collar bone, with small bite nibbles. I ran my hands down her sides and slid my hands in her waistband to slide her underwear off. I wanted to feel her. She adjusted her body to allow me to remove them, I removed them and she took her seat once again. I wrapped my one arm around her torso and grabbed her breast as she's grinding in to me. I could tell in her head she was deep in this pussy and I was enjoying every stroke she was giving. My nipples became extremely hard. As I softly firmly massaged and squeezed her breast while she stroke and rode my pussy real good. You know I want some. As she said it, I just let her know. Baby you can have any thing you want.

She unmounted me played with my nipples which arched the shii out my back and her hand ended up in between my legs and she slid her fingers in she exhaled. And if I'm not mistaken she said "thank you, for keeping it tight for me", which made my pussy jump mad crazy. I began looking and searching for her wet pussy as we finally positioned ourselves to be in one another at the same time. This shit was turning me on so mad crazy. I could tell the orgasm was going to be crazy. And, I wanted her to find the spot to make it erupt and trigger my orgasm............she whispered in my ear.

"Pak can I fuck you…. Can I take this pussy… can I fuck ur pussy and come on it?"
She had me feeling like some one of a type of nut, but for her, I mustard up the courage to say a soft
"Yes." in return. "You can have some…."

LETTING THE PAINT DRY

Phone rang as I was at the stop light, I selected "answer the phone" through the steering wheel,

"Hey are you home?"

"… In about 20 minutes, why what's up?"

I still had trust issues, asking me, was I home always sound like a set up to be burglarized. But, I didn't think that her motives were of any sort.

"O ok, I seen your text and I was at my cousin's, so I stopped passed, I was going to the store, down the street. Did you feel like company?"

"I don't mind, that's fine, I'll be there in a minute."

"Ok, going to the store, do you want some dumb chocolate ice cream?"

"Um chocolate ice cream is the best ice cream in thee world and you should just give it its props. But no, I just came from the gym, can you grab me some trail mix and a beef stick and a water please."

"Sure."

I'd forgotten that I'd text her. I got real nervous, but, is what it is. Fifteen minutes went pass but there was a truck hosing down the street which made my eta about ten minutes longer than I expected. She called back when I was about five minutes away, and I told her that I was close and that there was something that happened in the street. Gave her the code I use to let others in my apartment. And told her,

"You can wait for me inside the apartment."

She asked

"Are you sure, I can wait in the hallway."

I assured her that it was fine and that I was extremely close. About two minutes from the garage. Told her to make herself comfortable. And, that I would be there shortly.

She said "ok,"

I pulled up to the garage about 2 minutes after we hung up, went thru the arm to get in the garage, went up to about the second level of the parking garage and parked the car. Grabbed my bag and my back pack and headed to the elevator. Headed to the elevator. Called her to let her know I was coming through the door.

"Markie. I'll be walking through the door, getting off of the elevator now."

She said ok, and asked Do you want me to unlock the door?

I told her.

"I already unlock the door through the phone."

She replied with.

"My little geek."

"Um ok I chuckled, I walked through the door as I chuckled again."

I put my bags on the floor and the mail on the table.

She said.

"Hello."

It was a little awkward moment, probably where a hug or kiss went but just an awkward moment. I said hello back. And chuckled.

"Um Pak, what do you have on?"

She asked as she handed me the things I asked her to get from the store.

I looked at myself as I ripped open the beef jerky.

"Gym clothes."

"I didn't know you wore that at the gym?"

"What gym clothes?"

"Yeah, gym clothes?"

"I guess."

"I guess."

"What did you call me for the other day?"

I really didn't want to answer the question, it wasn't anything big but I felt like it was making me a tad vulnerable.

"I just called, because you said I never called, so you kind of came to mind so I called.

"O ok. you sound a little weird in the message, like you were upset about something. I thought my cousin said something to you."

"Oh no, I actually haven't seen your cousin, can I grab a shower right fast?"

"Sure."

"Radio on."

Sweet lady was on Tyerese, the west coast buhl.

"Pak, you have a little nice tight little ass in the yoga shorts. And you know you showing camel toe?"

"Um, ok."

"No, I'm serious, I had no clue that is how you went to the gym, thought you were more of a ball shorts boi."

"Oh, I am, today was a stretch day and I wear tights to stretch in. I was taking my shirt off as she came to the room door."

"Can I come in?"

"I'm not in the shower yet."

"That's ok, I don't mind."

I know we had been intimate but I didn't know where I was with just being nude in front of one another.

"Um sure."

"Pak, are you embarrassed to be in front of me naked."

"Um nahwl, not like a body insecure way, just not use to people and me being naked in my house. That is all."

"O ok. Well it's not a big deal ok."

"Um ok."

I grabbed the towel and put my ball shorts on and walked to the bathroom.

"Did you really put shorts on?"

"Yeah."

"Ok, Pak."

I took a shower for a minute about twenty minutes, she'd turned the tv on and the radio off about time I got out of the shower. I showered, dried off and put on ball shorts and a tee. I came out of the bathroom.

"Pak?"

"Yes?"

"I need a favor?"

"A favor?

"Yes, a favor."

"Do you have to work this weekend?"

"No, I am off actually for the next 5 days, unless I have an impromptu scheduling."

"Oh, ok."

"Can I stay here this weekend while my place gets painted?"

"Um…"

I was thrown for a loop and had no idea actually what to think I hesitated for a few seconds and responded with a sure, I don't think there's much food in the fridge but sure that's not a problem.

"Ok, thank you."

"Markie."

"Yes, Pak."

"I'm a little boring, and I am not sure if I know if I can keep you occupied during the weekend but you are more than welcome to make yourself at home and sure you can stay the weekend."

'Thank you Pak."

"You welcome. Did you want dinner?"

"Not right now, perhaps we can cook or order later. Just do what you usually do."

I actually wasn't about to do much the next day is my down time, I probably was going to stretch for a little while and catch up on tv shows."

"Ok, you fine, you can stretch."

"I'll go in the living room, you can watch tv. I usually stretch with music."

"Radio on."

I said as I walked to the living room.

I rolled up an el and began stretching, I was doing hamstrings stretches when I looked up.

"Would you like for me to stretch you?"

Apart of me was screaming yes and the dumb part of me was saying.

"No, I am ok."

"No, let me stretch you." she replied.

She walked over and told me.

"Lay back."

I hated moments like that, I got excited extremely quick especially when she was around.

As she started stretching me the music started playing, "none of your friends business" by Genuine.

"Pak, why are you so uptight?"

"Markie, I don't know."

"Dang you act like we are strangers."

"It's not that."

"Then, what is it Pak?"

"What?"

"What is it like? Why you so extra tense all the time?"

"Look it is what it is…"

She started rubbing the knot out of my hamstring.

"Oh my God, how were you even stretching the way you were, your hamstring is so tight."

"Pak, I told my cousin we were messing around."

"Oh ok."

"Is that ok with you?"

"There's not much of a problem there."

"Pak, what did you call me for the other day?"

She started rubbing very close to the base of my leg close to where my private parts and my legs connect. I almost started to enjoy what she was doing?

"Um Markie, did you want me to order something?"

"Sure soon, tell me why you called me."

"I got up to go to the kitchen."

"Pak, don't run from me."

"I'm not, I'm ordering for you."

"Ok, but after you order, we will finish the conversation."

I tried to prolong the moment by a little extension looking at the menu extra thoroughly. I wasn't at all sure about discussing my feelings. I dialed the phone and ended up ordered shrimp in a basked and a bacon cheese burger platter and some buffalo wings and some wine coolers and beers.

"Do you want a bacon cheese burger?"

She "nodded her head."

"Now that you've ordered for an army. Why'd you call me the other day?"

"I called you because I had a night mare about us arguing. And it bothered me so I called."

"Yeah?"

"Yeah."

"You called me at the same exact moment of me thinking of you and staying here while the apartment was being painted."

"Pak."

She pressed me against the counter.

"I like you."

I felt a little like a little bitch but at the same time, I felt comfortable with her aggression.

"Um, ok."

"Do you like me?"

"Do I like you?"

"Yes, do you like me? Do you like that my body is against yours right now. Because my body is going crazy."

I looked away.

"It doesn't matter."

"What does, it doesn't matter mean?"

She grabbed my chin and told me.

"Talk to me."

"Look, Markie it's cool, you got it."

"Pak, what the hail does that mean …?"

"Nothing."

"Can I kiss you?"

"Can you kiss me, why are you tripping?"

"I'm going to stop asking.

She just kissed me.

I fought it for a few seconds but melted as soon as she kissed me, my nipples were already getting hardened from the aggression of the conversation she squeezed my breast.

"You wearing fucking yoga shorts to the gym, showing that little dunk you got."

"Can I have you Pak. Pak can I have you?"

"What?"

"You heard me, can I have you?"

"Whatever."

"Why you can't never answer the questions I ask though."

"I mean to… as I looked directly in her eyes... be honest I am extremely taken off guard with all of this."

"Why, why are you taken off guard Pak?"

"Markie, I'm not sure like, a minute ago you just ask to chill while the crib is being painted, I am not going to lie, I definitely think about you, but I never think of anyone with relationships. I mean I am a bit socially inept. So, I just never thought of you any further than whatever length I could think of you to and it wasn't much serious. I tend to push my feelings aside."

"So, I'm saying though, I like you and I want to fuck with you."

"You like me, and you want to fuck with me. What does that mean?

"Pak I'm saying you fucking with some one?"

"What does, am I fucking with someone mean Markie?

"Are you fucking other bitches, have you fucked another bitch since we fucked?"

"Um ok, whoa. You have to excuse me two hours ago I thought I was chilling and about to smoke and parlay until I had a meeting.

"So, you don't want to talk about this?"

"Well technically I think you are a niguh probably. I don't think that I could really fuck with you, why do you even want to fuck with me for any ways and where did any of this come from."

"To be honest with you, I didn't even expect to have this conversation with you, then I really got type a little mad with you out and about with your workout clothes on. I mean I think intended on fucking you today but... I didn't expect this conversation..."

"Pak, what is it that you want in life?"

"Yo your tripping Markie, look I'm going to roll another el and wait for the food to be delivered."

I walked in to the room quite confused at the situation and my feelings on the situation.

I started rolling up and the doorbell rang, I walked out but she was already paying for the food.

I came out the room and shook my head and put the money on the table.

"I don't want that."

"You're company."

"I don't want that."

"You're company."

I became thoroughly confused with the current moment. She put the food in the kitchen. I started to the bedroom thought that would be a bad message to send at the moment, I was actually just trying to escape the moment, not necessarily go in to the bedroom did an about face turn and headed to the living room.

My phone went off and I didn't know if this was going to be an escape I needed or make the situation first.

She picked up my phone and I was mentally in the beginning stages of saying whoa when she just handed the phone to me. I was thankful that it was just the office reminder there was a conference next week. I listened and hung up the phone. And continued to the couch.

"I have to go get clothes, would you like to ride with me?"

"Um, no I'll be here."

"Can you ride with me?"

"I reservedly mumbled out a, um yea."

"You don't have to," she said.

Yet, I knew if I didn't, we were going to need to talk about it, I felt. Let me just put on some sweats. I went to the bed room. And, really lit my el up and was thinking of the moment. My feelings were so confused. Happy, sad. Excited. Frustrated. It didn't stop with those I was internally emotionally in a frenzy. I threw on some jeans with a smedium hoodie. Pushed up the sleeves and fixed the hoodie, pulled the strings and tied the strings.

We walked to her car and headed to her place.

"Pak?"

"Yes, Markie?"

"Are you seeing someone?"

"Am I seeing someone? I have friends and situations."

"What the fuck is friends and situations…?"

"…what the fuck is a question, you don't want to know the answer to."

"You mad difficult."

It was pretty much quiet for the rest of the way to her place. We pulled up and park, she asked was I coming in, but it wasn't really a question more like an expectation, so I said,

"Sure."

We walked in to the house. She said.

"You can have a seat. You know Pak, I understand and get manners but really? Just really, I know you can't be like this with everyone.

She made me feel sad inside. I hated being like this and I can't tell you why I am like this. Possibly if she liked me the way she says she do the walls must go up, but they may come down. Not on purpose but, practice what you preach. I really was truly caught off guard with all of this emotional conversation.

I sat down and crossed my legs as she went to grab her overnight things. To be honest with you I didn't even know.

As I felt confident with my thoughts.

"You know Markie, you know I don't know you know you, like I have no idea what you do. I don't even think I know your real name. I don't even think I think you know my real name."

Her phone rang just as she was about to respond.

"Can you see what it says."

I really didn't want to, I really didn't want to know anyone who called her phones, their name or make any speculation. I mean did she really know what she was truly asking for. People seem to interrupt you in your life when you are at your points and nodes.

I walked over to the phone. It says "Ma."

"Can you hand that to me please."

I handed her the phone.

She selected to answer the phone.

"What's up Ma? Aiyte ma I'll be right there. Did you call road side assistance?"

I was actually looking at her wall it was filled with photographs.

"Pak, I hope you don't mind, but I need to go wait with my mom with road side assistance."

"You can wait here, I can call you a car or you can come with…"

"Ok, I don't mind. But I see you one of those."

"One of those what?"

"Escapades."

"Yo this my moms though."

"I know, I ain't saying too much but yeah…"

"Aiyte Pak."

We walked out of the house as she locked the house, she said.

"Maybe you could put one of your systems on my house."

"Yea, maybe. It wouldn't be a problem, if you really want one."

We walked to the car. And got in to the car we pulled off. She put her hand on my thigh, Pakira don't be like that.

I didn't really have anything to say.

We drove for about 15 minutes and then pulled up behind her mother's luxury SUV. She left her hazards on and walked to her mother's car and put her hazard lights on. They spoke for a little while, she made a call and then they came to the car. I got out the car as they started towards the car. Mom Pakira, Pakira that's my mom Mrs. Marks

Her mom replied with.

"Oh, you got another one."

"Ma!"

"How you doing baby?"

"Im fine ma'am, um Markie, I am going to take a look at the car."

"They said that there was going to be about forty-five minutes until road side assistance got here."

I changed the tire in about twenty minutes. I walked back to the car, said that.

"I changed the tire and the car is good to go."

"Thank you dear. Her mother said.

"At least you got one with a skill this time."

"Ma."

"What?"

"Nothing."

"Meet me at the car dealer ship in the morning."

"And, again thank you dear. Don't let her boss you around."

"No problem ma'am. And yes, Mrs. Marks."

She walked her mother back to the car and then return back to the car. She watched her mother pull off and then she pulled off directly after her.

"Thank you for changing my mother's tire Pak."

I think she really liked that.

"It wasn't a problem."

We drove towards my house. They beeped and parted ways at about two blocks.

"You know you could have waited for road side assistance."

"I know, it wasn't nothing."

"Thank you, I appreciate you doing that. Look at you you got car gunk all over your hands."

She reached over in to the glove compartment and handed me cleaning wipes for my hands. We reached my apartment in about twenty minutes. We parked in the parking lot. Her cousin was pulling out at the same time.

"Did you still need the key for the weekend, I'll be in Chicago it is in the mail box if you need it cousin. And your mother said call her when you get in she just called me."

"Ok, I might need it, I don't think so though, but thanks. Be good be safe. I'll make sure I get it out the mail box."

"I just seen my mom."

"I know she was asking me a million and one questions." She looked in my direction, so I guess I was the topic.

Her cousin shook her head at us and left out of the parking lot.

She pulled in to the parking spot and parked the car. We got out of the car, grabbed her things and went towards the elevator, we didn't say much towards one another. Everything was a bit awkward. We boarded the elevator and went up towards the apartment and went in towards the apartment. I put my food in the microwave.

"Would you like for me to put any of your food in the microwave."

"Yes, please."

Ok, it's in the microwave. I have to take a shower to get the car residue off of me.

"I understand Pak."

I showered and put my shorts and slides back on. She was eating her burger when I got back to the living room.

"You are an interesting person Pak."

"I guess Markie."

"Why are you so standoffish."

"I don't think that I am."

"You have this huge chip on your shoulder that is beyond measuring, why?"

"I don't."

"You do."

"Ok, well, enjoy your food."

I grabbed my food out of the microwave sat down at my desk and began working on some things on my desk top. I'd been working on some new code and I really needed to clear my mind.

"Pak?"

"Yes Markie?"

"I'm sorry."

"You're sorry."

"I apologize."

"Ok."

"That's all that you are going to say?"

"Well to be honest, what are you apologizing for?"

"I mean maybe I handle things wrong, maybe I came off wrong. I just I don't know when you came in the apartment earlier, I really got angry. I really, I can't even explain if it was it angered me. I just didn't like you walking around like that and single. And, I need to put a stop to it, that is how I felt. I think I understand you more than you think some one could, I am not sure why but that is how I feel. Can I grab a shower?"

"Sure."

I was glad the conversation had ended because I had no clue as to how to respond. I actually had fixed a piece of code that I'd been trying to fix for a couple of days now, she spent about thirty minutes in the shower. I think to be honest I'd got lost in the code.

When she came out she looked cute as all heck, I was still mad stuck between my feelings though. I looked up and said,

"Oh, you look cute."

She said.

"Thank you."

She asked.

"Are you going to bed soon."

I told her.

"I'm not sure that I may just end up sleeping on the couch or something, I was really in to my code."

"I'd really like for you to sleep in the bed Pak."

"Ok, I'll be to bed Markie."

I spent another hour and forty-five minutes coding. I saved the projects I was working on, hit the lights to the low setting and went up to the bed. She was reading a book, I ain't gone lie I found that to be type sexy

"Thank you, for coming up to bed."

I slid off my slides and got in the bed.

"Goodnight." she said.

"Good night." I replied.

"Pak."

"Yes Markie?"

"Hold me."

"Hold you?"

"Yes, hold me."

I turned her direction and wrapped my arms around her.

"Goodnight."

"Goodnight."

I think we both fell asleep thinking about a lot, next thing I knew she was on the phone with her mother telling her mother she'd be there by nine. It was about seven fifteen, after I squinted to adjust my just opening eyes. Grabbed the remote and turned the television on.

"I have to meet my mom. Are you going to be here?"

"Yes, I'll be here."

"Ok, I will be back."

"Ok, have a good day."

I laid in the bed for a little while longer. I really thought to myself, how I got in this situation. I think the thing with social activities there's a balance of energy that is needed. And most people I imagine go in to a social setting less aware of that. But yeah. I got up made some French toast and got back to coding. I was behind on a personal project. Kind of similar to the concept of holograms. Mine kind of a 3d virtual concept type. I coded for awhile and ended up falling asleep with my laptop on the bed.

I was awakened by some one sitting on my back rubbing and kissing my back and shoulders. She felt me waking up and she leaned down.

"I really appreciate you yesterday, you fixing my mom's car."
She gave me enough room to flip my body over.

"It was no problem at all."
She started whispering in my ear.

"I really really appreciate you fixing my mom's car."
I chuckled. And my phone rang. I reached and got my phone.

"Hey Brendon, yeah that's fine, ok sure. See you Monday afternoon. Probably just watch some sports. Ok nah, order a pitcher for me. Ok, have a great night bro."
She was still kissing me. I had to get to coding though, now that I had a Monday meeting. It wasn't mandatory, but it was just going to put me ahead of the curve. Her kisses felt real nice she was so soft.

I brought some things for dinner if you wanted to cook something with me.

"Oh, I really need to be coding now that I have this meeting on Monday. How about I make a deal with you. I sit there while you cook, and I'll try very hard to fix this bug. And, I'll splurge for the movies tomorrow."

"Ok, since it is work related, I really wanted to make dinner with you."

"Looks like we'll get the chance to make a few dinners together.

"You think? I need another part of the deal as she leaned down and kissed me."

"What is that Markie?"

She put her hands in my short and rubbed my clit so soft.

"I want some of you."

"You want some of me?"

I chuckled, as I did, you could feel my clit harden.

She felt it and said "mmmmm, I want some."

"You want some?"

I took her hand and placed her fingers inside of me. For some reason I was never the type to be able to be ok with the verbal fem responses.

"Is that what you want?" I asked.

"You want some of that?"

"Yes, can I have some of that?"

"What you gone do with it?"

"Imma make it leak all over the place, imma make it come hard. Imma rub my dyck all against them walls."

"Yeah? Well it seems like you do a lot of talking."

"Talk that shit now. Make sure when I come right back you talking that shit."

She went and put on her strap. And, she came back.

"I got us something new to work with?"

"Oh yeah."

She finished fastening the sides to the harness, she climbed back on and straddled me. She put her strap in between my breast.

"They are just so huge. You not gone suck the head my dyck."

She stopped stroking my titties, and rubbed the tip of her dyck on my lips and asked me to open my mouth.

"Can you suck it please."

I wanted to and didn't want to at the same time. I liked her and wanted to please her and I didn't mind it actually turned me on. But at the same time, I just felt like it, it looked and it feels so gay. I grabbed her dick and sucked mostly the head real good. I put my thumb in her pussy and massaged her pussy as I sucked her strapped like it was natural, she almost slobbered. She pushed me back up on the bed and turned me around. She shoved my shoulders to pin them to the mattress and adjusted my ass in the air and the bottoms of my feet touching one another. She started slapping the top of my ass crack with her fat meat. She slapped my ass with her plastic meat then she rubbed my pussy hole with her hardened dick tip, she rubbed it real firmly above my pussy hole then slid deep in to my pussy.

"Pak you never really let anyone fuck you, before have you? Have you?"

As she shoved herself deep in to me.

"No."

She slapped my ass cheeks and she leaned back.

"Can I fuck this pussy?"

"Huh?"

She started slow stroking my pussy. My pussy wanted to stay closed and wanted to relax at the same time. And she was going to force it to relax, she rubbed my back as she stroked the pussy. I felt her dick vibrating inside me.

"Damn you excited for me. Aren't you?"

She tilted her head back.

"You feel that. Your pussy can't lie and neither can mine."

She started aggressively pounding my pussy. She put her thumb in my ass and was fucking my ass hole with her thumb, she was stroking my pussy good. I couldn't help but to start fucking her dick back.

"Who you keeping this pussy tight for. Why you so stingy?"

The more I fucked her back the deeper her dick would get and the vibration of the strap would open my pussy up regardless if I wanted it to open or not. I started leaking all over her thighs.

"Damn your pussy is so fucking wet."

She was still pounding my pussy. And, as she pounded my pussy, she was grabbing and rubbing my nipples. She turned me over and laid me on my back and just stroked me until I came all over strap. She came after the convulsions of my orgasm, making my pussy jump sending vibrations signals to the plug end of the strap she had inside of her. She let out a loud.

"Damn, this tight pussy making me come."

She was still stroking my pussy when I stopped her, took her strap off her laid on my back open my legs put as much as her pussy inside of mine that I could get inside of mine and let her grind until we came. She was sucking on my tits so good the entire time. Her pussy was so wet from me dripping all over it. She slapped my thighs bent down and bit them. And said she was going to cook dinner. I sat up on the bed and told her.

"I'm going to get you back later."

"I know daddi, I know."

"Oh ok, as long as you know."

"That pussy good though."

I squinted and shook my head.

"Imma grab a shower."

I figured I'd get her back now and later. For some reason for the most part sex for me was a competition, and that fact that she just only came once, well it wasn't going to sit right with me.

I waited for about 5 minutes and I snuck in to the shower behind her grabbed her by the waist and put my pelvic area on the back of her bare ass. I grabbed her breast and squeezed them.

"You swear you want this pussy."

"I do."

"You do, huh?"

"Yelp."

I turned her around and started sucking on her nipples exciting them to the extreme. I reached down and her clit was so hard for me. I sat on the edge of the tub and put her leg over my shoulder and feasted on her pussy like it was grandma's Thanksgiving meal. I teased her pussy lips with my tongue then pushed my tongue in between what had become her swollen vagina lips. I sucked on her clit and lips simultaneously for a little while. I wanted that clit in my mouth badly it was so hard. She grabbed my hair and couldn't help but deep slow stroke my mouth with her hard clitoris. She started scratching my back and holding my head. She fucked my mouth so good until her wet juices camouflaged themselves with the warm running shower.

"Damn Pak, I really like when your mouth is on me."

I sucked on her nipples a little more as she intermittently let out an enjoying mmm I kissed her neck kissed her. We grabbed wash clothes and washed one another. Took a shower for another fifteen minutes then met up in the kitchen after she was getting ready to cook and me doing some coding. She put on some early time music poured some wine and started cooking.

I rolled my el got my cran-grape juice and got to coding. We cooked and coded for the hour and forty-five-minute, dinner was ready. We decided I would not code while I ate and we would have a conversation.

DO I HAVE TO ASK TWICE?

Phone was ringing, I think I'd just hit rem sleep, if that's what deep sleep is called, you know. 2:14 am before I slide the slider to answer the call. The display on the screen reads "unlisted." I clear my throat and flop my head back in the pillow, "Hello."

"Hello, um why do I have to call you?"

"Who is this?"

"You know who this is."

"Oh."

"Ok."

"Come see me."

"Come see you huh?"

"Yeah."

"Yeah?"

"Yeah ok, it's 2:17 in the morning."

"Do I have to ask twice?"

"Nawhl, I'm on the next train out, and that sounded like a demand and not a request."

"Ok, I'll see when you get here. I shouldn't have to demand or request twice."

"You sure will. And, whatever."

"See you soon then."

"Ok, text me the address."

A text came through on my phone.

"Got it, as I replied after the alert came through."

"See you soon, yes." She said.

"Yes, see you soon."

The call disconnected. And I, drifted for about three minutes. Popped my head up and looked at the clock, it was 2:28. I looked up the train departures. There was one leaving at 3:45 which would put me there a little before 6. I grabbed an athletic bag, threw some clothes in there, I'd change on the train. I hopped in the shower. And headed to the train station. I got there in about twenty minutes, had about 9 minutes until the train pulled off, and I definitely planned to go to sleep.

The train stations announcement pulled up just as I found a seat. Announcing the train pulling in and boarding. I walked down to the train and the train was pulling in it took about a good 3 minutes to stop and break and unload. Then the on-loading passengers were boarding. Scanned my ticket and found a 3-seater, because I was definitely about to be stretched out. Threw my bag against the window end of the seat and laid with my head using it as a pillow. The conductor walked passed and nodded, I responded with a morning and laid down on the chair. There weren't many passengers. But I've taken this ride before around this time, and there usually aren't. I thought it was quite odd to receive the call but went with it, I didn't mind it. Just knew it was for a moment and nothing serious.

Drifted off to sleep and about an hour and 30 minutes later I hear the announcement of my stop coming in 10 minutes.

I sit up and stretch. A good needed stretch. And I unzip my gym sports bag. And start to change my clothes. Took off my t shirt and put on a shirt. Then looked around and changed my sweat pants to some denim jeans. I changed my clothes in about 5 minutes and just waited for the train to reach my destination.

V neck and some jeans with some polo buckle ankle boots. I had so grown out of my fitted stage. But sometimes very much wanted to wear them. Always never wanted to be that old buhl dagger… as I thought about my thoughts, I heard the.

"Now pulling in…signal."

Threw the LV sports duffle strap over my head and went to hail a cab. As I walked to the cab station I always remembered the story of uncle I think Aaron being a cab company back in the day down here. Or near here. You know when you don't live somewhere the things that are far are close. I pulled up the address on the phone as I open the cab door sat down, passed the driver the phone. The driver read the address and put it in the gps, 17 minutes in a deep Indian accent. Oh wow, ok. I texted her.

"In a cab, on my way."

After that, I just took in some of the scenery. I'd like traveling, I like seeing different cultures and different history of how things were built. I appreciated seeing those things in person. I didn't come here as often as I liked, but I don't get to travel as much either.

"Long day" the cabbie said.

"Um no, not really, and you?"

"Oh no, my day is just beginning."

"Oh, ok that makes sense. How are Sundays?"

"How is the cab business. With the new car services"?

"Oh, yea for our customers that we have always had it is the same."

I waited for about 5 minutes and I snuck in to the shower behind her grabbed her by the waist and put my pelvic area on the back of her bare ass. I grabbed her breast and squeezed them.

"You swear you want this pussy."

"I do."

"You do, huh?"

"Yelp."

I turned her around and started sucking on her nipples exciting them to the extreme. I reached down and her clit was so hard for me. I sat on the edge of the tub and put her leg over my shoulder and feasted on her pussy like it was grandma's Thanksgiving meal. I teased her pussy lips with my tongue then pushed my tongue in between what had become her swollen vagina lips. I sucked on her clit and lips simultaneously for a little while. I wanted that clit in my mouth badly it was so hard. She grabbed my hair and couldn't help but deep slow stroke my mouth with her hard clitoris. She started scratching my back and holding my head. She fucked my mouth so good until her wet juices camouflaged themselves with the warm running shower.

"Damn Pak, I really like when your mouth is on me."

I sucked on her nipples a little more as she intermittently let out an enjoying mmm I kissed her neck kissed her. We grabbed wash clothes and washed one another. Took a shower for another fifteen minutes then met up in the kitchen after she was getting ready to cook and me doing some coding. She put on some early time music poured some wine and started cooking.

I rolled my el got my cran-grape juice and got to coding. We cooked and coded for the hour and forty-five-minute, dinner was ready. We decided I would not code while I ate and we would have a conversation.

DO I HAVE TO ASK TWICE?

Phone was ringing, I think I'd just hit rem sleep, if that's what deep sleep is called, you know. 2:14 am before I slide the slider to answer the call. The display on the screen reads "unlisted." I clear my throat and flop my head back in the pillow, "Hello."

"Hello, um why do I have to call you?"

"Who is this?"

"You know who this is."

"Oh."

"Ok."

"Come see me."

"Come see you huh?"

"Yeah."

"Yeah?"

"Yeah ok, it's 2:17 in the morning."

"Do I have to ask twice?"

"Nawhl, I'm on the next train out, and that sounded like a demand and not a request."

"But yes, business is different."

I said "Yea, I can imagine with some of those services you can have a ride in 3 minutes. I used a cab the other day and waited literally almost an hour if not."

"Oh, sorry to hear that, where were you?"

"Oh, I wasn't here."

"Oh, I see."

I left it at that, it was an awkward ending like most of my conversations, but it was because I'd definitely began to ponder this little trip.

Our Connection was interesting. I wasn't even supposed to fall fo shawtie. She was just supposed to drop some gems I needed. But, why, right? why wouldn't I? …As I chuckled about the forth, or the possible forth coming moments. I really didn't have any expectations nor hopes. I knew I'd like to make sure my word is bond, we'd discussed a few business prospects, maybe she enjoyed my business planning and wanted to hear some more of my ideas, or possibly, you know, I think some females for whatever weird reason enjoy my company. Although I am a heck of an introvert, I usually have no clue as to why some women take to me. But hey we all need someone right.

I sat there and thought for the rest of the ride with my head up towards the ceiling of the car. Most say I think too much, it makes me think how little others think, and what is "not thinking" like. I remember a few years back wanting to grab an apartment out here with a homie at the time we were coming out here every weekend. But one of those mishaps of trying to do something with someone opposed of just going after it myself.

The cabbie started to slow down and look for the address, he hit the brakes a little hard after almost passing the house. Turned the meter off. And, said "$28.32."

"Good lord. $28.32 where'd we ride from China, sike nah, here you go" gave him $35. I know it probably wasn't like the tips he got but a $6 dollar tip is a lot for me. I cracked a smile and he cracked a smile "have a good day ma'am."

"You too, hope your day be prosperous."

"Oh, why thank you." He said a bit surprisingly.

I got out of the cab and had some thoughts of that interaction with the cabbie on my mind. Like, I always found it odd that people are shocked at encouraging words or that I can speak some other languages. I don't know why that shocks people. Which I definitely need to study my language. It's a beautiful thing to be able to communicate with many. Something I can't say I pride myself in it because I would know more, but I appreciate that I take an interest in different languages and communication styles.

The cabbie pulls off. I softly stomp my feet to make my pants hang over my boots correctly. I shake my hair to make sure it lays in a way that I feel confident.
Adjusted the shoulder strap on my duffle bag and walked up to the door. Door was a bit husky. Just wanted to look cute at our first moment. I was feeling a bit onset anxiety, but we took some deep breaths and rang the doorbell "bing bang bing bing pause bing bing bing bing bong." The door opens up shortly after the bell after that all I seen was…

"The smile." I hate my smile so I lowered my head softly cheese smiled and shook my head. Had to wipe my eyebrow for whatever reason. So, I was unaware if she was aware that my birthstone is emerald. I wondered that because she came to the door in an emerald silk lace type of situation, that just made me wonder even more what was about to go down. But then again I'm just not around women who dress sexy just because. So, I didn't want to take any of this personal.

"Hey."

"Hey."

She kissed me on the cheek I leaned in to receive it. She tied her robe.

"Um, you know I could have come get you. Can you take off your shoes?"

I really didn't know what that meant from home or from the train station. I just replied with

"Oh nawl, it's cool" and removed my shoes.

She chuckled and took my bag and put it on the bannister, I actually cringed of the tension that it was putting on the shoulder strap of the duffle bag, and I know I was going to be anal about it.

"So, um, you can put that on the floor." She put it on the little piece of step that curves the bottom of the stair case. And scooted down the hall, while asking "are you hungry?"

"I could go for something to eat, sure."

She led us to the kitchen.

She had the things to keep the food warm they were covered with clear tops, you could see French toast, home fries and sausage patties. She walked to the cabinet and took two plates down and brought them over to the table along with some cutlery. Then, I watched her walk to the refrigerator to get juice and water and some glasses out the cabinet. And, bring them back to the table.

"We both can't be shy"

She awkwardly positioned herself across from me. Awkward because conversation was going to be so direct.

"Shy, nawhl, I'm not shy shy, but you can carry the conversation though."

"How was your ride?"

"It was cool, slept most of the way really. Probably dry mouth, wide open. But, hey sleep is sleep and good sleep is good sleep."

"Yeah, I guess so."

"You guess, oh yeah, I enjoy my rest … work hard, play hard, rest hard. I'm a firm believer

in sleep, gives time for the body to rejuvenate so you know go figure."

"You shocked I called you?"

"You shocked I came?"

She put the juice in front of me for me to open and fixed our plates, she sat down.

"Shocked? I don't know about shocked, kinda liked that you called, if that means anything.

I'm not going to lie I very rarely lie about my emotions, and I can only answer questions

with the answers I have even if they don't seem like the answer or connected to the

question."

"That's fair" she responded.

I very rarely inquired about feelings. The thought of asking did she like that I came, to her

crossed my thoughts, but I left it alone. I poured the syrup on the French toast and asked for some

butter, she pointed to the refrigerator. I awkwardly got up and walked to the silver refrigerator she

said "on the shelf" it was right there, I got it and sat back down. Spread some on my French toast.

Food looked good, I was hungry but not hungry hungry. But, it was my favorite, so how could I not

indulge.

"Sooo" as I sat down "can I ask, why did you call me?"

Grabbed her hands and said grace.

"Lord, thank you for this meal, thank you for the resources and the skills to prepare this meal.

And, may others be blessed, the way you have blessed us. Amen."

"Amen."

"Why?"

"If you don't have an answer it's fine. Just you not no set-up artist. Niguhs ain't finnuh buss

in and rob niguh's and shii."

… she laughed, a bit too hard for my personal liking, I laughed too. "oh, that's funny?"

"Nahh, I don't do that."

"Oh, ok. "Cause a niguh only got like Bruce Lee Van Damme skills out this bii. But I'm going out with the Tiger Style."

"Oh, you Kareem Abdul Jabar huh."

I was shocked at her wit, it was cute though.

"Yes peaceful giant I am", she chuckled again.

I ate the French toast and like four sausage patties.

For some reason sausage patties fried hard kinda, definitely for me.

"The food is good."

"Thank you. Figured you'd be a little hungry once you got here."

"Thank you, that was kind of you, fo certain."

We finished up our food, she washed the dishes she was telling me how she had got some mail earlier this week and she'd just been in a pretty good mood. And she wanted to call me. She said she didn't question it much but she laughed at doing it and had no idea how I was going to respond.

She wiped down the sink and walked over to me, she was standing on the side of me. I turned and open my one leg and maneuvered it around her leg accidentally bumping her leg as of now she was standing in front of me. I took her hands. Shy I don't know if we were both shy or not but I was lost and confused. She looked at me and that drop feeling happened the one in the pit of your gut, the good one, not the bad one. I wasn't quite sure what to do, but knew what I'd like to do, and that's what I did. She had such full lips. I stuck a small portion of my tongue out and licked her lips and went in to a very slow seeking kiss, seeking for a response. I came out of the kiss and rubbed my lips on hers. Rubbed my forehead on her lips. I came completely out of the kiss, looked at her and asked her "why am I here?"

I damn sure didn't know, not really.

She very softly said "I needed you here" and looked at herself.

"Yeah?"

"Yeah."

I laid my face into the curve of her neck, she smelled so nice, a sweet scent. A fresh spring scents. I really didn't have any more words or I was going to talk myself out of the moment. I rubbed my cheek and nose against the side of her face, wrapped my arms around her waist. She put her hands in my back pockets we looked at one another and smiled. I chuckled and put my hand back on her chin and brought her lips to mine. I have a very bad habit of sucking on lips and mouths of women I like. I know, I enjoy it, it feels really nice in my mouth. But, I don't know how it feels to receive it, 'cause I'd probably be like, is this niguh sucking my mouth. Something very new… as I internally chuckled. I enjoyed her lips her mouth for a little while longer. I could tell she was letting me lead the way. I didn't really know where I was fittin' to lead us, but I was just fucking with it. I unbuckled my belt with one hand. And pulled her close to me … I took her hand and put it in my pants, I was uncertain her dominant hand or if she even knew the meaning of what I was doing, I was very excited and I wanted her to know that.

I took her hand and put it in the waistband of my boxers, took her finger and tandem-ly grazed my clit, and I softly said it's so hard, shii started jumping like the last minute of popping microwave popcorn. I placed her fingers inside of me and said it's tight.

She replied with a "yes" and her voice cracked, I smiled. I appreciated that. She started a motion, I stopped her motion with a firm grip of her wrist leaned to her ear and I asked.

"Rub it for me please."

She did just so, then stopped.

She took my hand and led me to her bedroom. We walked, I walked holding my pants by the belt. She turned the down stairs light off. As we hit the bottom steps and the upstairs lights came on, shii was some crazy techie shii on the low. I grabbed my bag and headed upstairs with her. We got to her bedroom.

I asked could I use her bathroom she pointed to the bathroom. I went to the bathroom and changed into some shorts and a tank top came back out. I pulled her into standing she'd sat on the bed. I asked was she sure. She softly said yes. I slowly pulled her robe belt to untie it. It open to a golden honey complexion. Put my nose back in the curve of her neck. I sat down on the bed and let her stand in front, I softly bit in between the area below her belly button. I paused and rubbed my face on hips. Her entire body smelled so nice. Her warmth as I held her made me want to just enjoy just feeling what she felt like in my arms. But I couldn't come off too corny, so I imagine I needed to get to putting it down, I backed on the bed and laid down. I positioned her in a top mountain climber position just for the moment, I rolled us over and had her arch her back so she her breast which had become erect were close enough to my mouth that I softly bit them through the fabric, she had some crazy probably Le'Pearla type shii on, lace with hooks, but was like a sports bra, but lingerie-y.

Definitely nice on her and accented her tits real nice, but the robe, it had to come off. She softly let out a sound when I bit each one. I was shocked she was enjoying me, and really had no clue of her expectations, ain't wanna fuck a bitch head up so I imagine I'd keep it simple. I ran my locs down the middle of her chest and across the top of her hardened nipples, rubbed my race with them and engulfed them with my mouth, enjoying them like they were ice cream packed in the cone, firm licking them with my tongue and my lips, my torso was in her crotch, she began grinding on me and placed her arms around the back of my neck. I broke out of the hug, her hands went to the side of her, I went to below her waste and stuck my nose in her private area. I came back up and laid on top of her and put my nose back in her neck, but close to her ear. And said

"Can I have some?"

"Yes."

"You gone give me some, you gone cum for me?"

Her voice cracked again with a "yes."

I softly firmly asked "you want me to fuck you?"

"She shook her head yes."

"Mmmm…"

I grind-ed my hips in to widen her legs, she felt me. I slid back down to her waist and removed the boy short type emerald bottoms, she had on, and pondered why was she so in sync with me. I tossed her leg over my shoulder and put my nose in her pussy to open her lips apart. I felt her clit on my nose and quickly put it in my mouth to feel how erect she was for me.

As I felt her a natural "mmmm" sound happened.

And a natural profanity word "shit" as I felt her on my tongue and licked the tip of her clit with the flat part of my tongue, trying to stimulate her more.

She managed to breath out an "oh" and a soft "fuck."

I curled my tongued for it to clip her pussy hole as I licked her. Licked around her pussy hole then kissed her clit. I placed my tongue on the base of her clit and sucked it softly, I didn't know if she responded to soft or hard but again I just wanted to enjoy and savor her. I could have licked her all night; my tongue really enjoyed her clit. She responded way earlier than I expected her to, I myself was so fuk'n turned on, it was so hard in my mouth. My tongue was determined to feel it, go soft, she just made my mouth salivate. I made love to her clit with my mouth for I think a good twenty minutes before she grabbed my head and started directing my head with my locs. She grabbed a hand full of hair and fucked my mouth firm, thrusted, I flickered the base of her clit and she let out a yelp kind of yell, I think it took her by surprise. She said "Shit" but kept grinding, I laid my head on her thigh and slowly entered her with my fingers. I wanted to see was she going to allow me, wanted me, resist me, need me. I tried to read what every millimeter of her depth meant. I rubbed her walls the way I liked mine rubbed. I asked her to say.

"Oooooh for me."

I could hear where the tone of her breath changed when I touched her spots. I started my out and in motion, while softly biting her thighs, but I wanted her clit back in my mouth, so as I used my fingers to stroke and rub her pussy I had taken her clit back in to my mouth and sucked it like your trying to get the last of the icee pop out of its plastic sleeve. I'd became hungry for her, she started riding my fingers back, I took my fingers out and came up to her mouth, she grabbed my face and kissed my mouth and licked my lips. I put my lips softly on her ears and asked.

"Can I go in?"

I knew she felt me on her leg. She reached down and guided me in, I slowly pushed deep in I felt the first circle, the second circle depth, and third where I was entirely deeply inside, asked her to take a deep breath and I slow long stroked her. She started soaking up the sheets.

"Damn baby, your pussy is wet for me though."

"Yes, you make this pussy feel good."

I had her knees on my shoulder stroking her slow, baby play with it for me. She rubbed her clit as I stroked it slow. I felt like I was getting harder and harder, I slow stroked her and then put it to the back and pulsated small short firm strokes. I wanted her to buss all over me, she excitedly started saying "yes."

I responded with an.

"Oh fuck"

'Cause not only was she dripping wet, I felt myself running down my leg. To be honest I was looking for this feeling. I found a rhythm and stuck with it until we both climaxed. I turned her over on her stomach and slid in her, she got on her knees and found her own rhythm, she used me until she found another orgasm, I was so turn on by her getting hers. She laid flat. I slid out of her and laid on the other side of the bed and placed the covers up to my waist.

I'd drifted off to sleep. I felt something on my waist band. She was unbuckling my harness. She slid her hand in between my legs.

"Mmm, baby why you still hard, huh? Can I have some? Can I have some of you? I don't want you to be hard though baby. How I make it go down?"

Her voice in my ear and her fingers on my clit I could barely get my windpipes to push out any sound.

"Are you hard for me? Do you want to be inside of me?"

She felt my clit jump when she said that and chuckled and said.

"Mmm…"

She put her fingers inside and said,

Oh my God, I can feel your heart beat so clear, you're throbbing so hard."

She grabbed my strap and was about to put it inside me.

I chuckled and said "what are you doing, oh nawhl."

"What I can't?

"I'm not saying you can't can't, but not with mine."

"Oh, you can be all up in me with it, but I can't be in you with it …"

"Nawhl, not this one you can't. Nawhl, just that's just not right, getting fuk'd by your own.

Now, if you were my girl and it was the only one I'd used on you or something sure.

"Ok whatever."

She smacked my pussy she was mad and was about to get up. When I pulled her towards me and placed her in a sitting position on top of me. I ran my hand up her torso in a slow manner and cupped her breast, squeezed them softly, she turned around and put my hand back on her breast and started riding me. She started riding me so hard. I think she was mad that I didn't let her fuck me but if she was going to fuck me like this I am glad I paused. But she started moaning. And that's when I realized she said,

"fuck" making me cum. she just got off again.

That shit just made me more fucking hard. She got up and walked naked to the bathroom. And turned the shower on and came back to the room and started putting her hair up.

"I have to go out for a while, you can stay here, or did you know when you were leaving?"

"Um, I can be out now that's fine."

"Don't be one of them Sig."

"What are you talking about?"

"I'll be back around two, can you be here when I get here?"

"Um I don't know, can you come here?"

She rolled her eyes and walked over. I put her hand back on my clit. And started her to rub it, it instantly became a Mexican jumping bean, it must have turned her on because the,

"mmm."

From her mouth seem like she'd considered forgiving me. I took her head and kissed her and she kissed me and rubbed my clit. In the middle of the kiss, I took her fingers and put them inside of me and squeezed them. And started rubbing my clit. She stopped kissing me and began sucking my nipple, I came in the next 96 seconds. Hard embarrassingly hard. She whispers a,

"Yes". And then she said.

Imma open that pussy up, and she smacked my shit again.

"I'm getting in the shower stingy."

I watched her walk back to the shower and was a bit concerned at coming for her especially while her fingers were inside of me. I don't think I liked being vulnerable like that for anyone. She got a shower and got dressed. Let me know there was food in the refrigerator or menus in the drawer to order. She left for the day. Said she'd be back.

She came back around 3pm in the middle of me stretching.

"How are you?" She said when she came in,

"I'm cool."

"How are you?"

"I'm good."

"Would like to pick up where we left off.

I'd been working out so I needed a shower.

I responded with,

"That's possible, let me just grab a shower."

She said,

"Perhaps I'll join you."

"That's fine."

She walked upstairs and I picked up the things I had on the floor and came up shortly after her. She'd started the shower and started undressing, I looked at her for a while, while she undressed. She was so feminine without even trying. Women like that always impressed me. I never hated being a woman, just hated what came with being a woman. The oppression, the cat calling, the discrimination. But there are certain women that know how to play the game. Even in hip hop. Why I like the female rapper Nicki Minaj. Although she was a rapper she played it as a woman, and I think that is why she is so successful, she understood sex sell she understood the assignment. I just don't know how to advertise sexy with also being prepared to take the oncoming energy.

She was cute and beautiful. Some times that can be a rare combination. Not all females can pull off cute. She'd got to the last piece of clothing as I watched her go in the shower. I then took off my ball shorts boxer briefs, sports bra and basketball jersey, my regular in the house wear. And followed her to the shower. I must have enjoyed last night or this morning more than I knew.

My body wanted to touch her, but, knew it was going to be immediately excited. The water was warm. As it ran over her body, I opened the door to the shower and stepped in. I took the sponge off the drying rack and began to lather it. I washed her back softly. Wiped over her buttocks and her legs. Turned her around washed around her neck over her breast, her front torso. And she opened her legs for me to wash in-between her legs. I gently rubbed her in-between her legs and down her legs. She grabbed the wash cloth that she'd given me. And let it get wet, she lathered it and washed me down. We rinsed off and kissed. We washed one another one more time then washed ourselves and then got out of the shower. I got out of the shower and then handed her a towel when she got out of the shower.

She grabbed the lotion off of the bathroom sink, and headed to the room, I grabbed some shorts from my bag and threw them on. And sat on the bed. With shorts and a sleeve-less tee on. She started lotion-ing.

"You want me to do that?"

"Oh, I wouldn't mind."

She walked over to in front of me, I squeezed a strawberry lemon citrus type of lotion in my hand and rubbed it in my hand and then applied it to her legs. I'm not going to lie I tried to do it as sensual as possible, I wanted her to know the touch of my hands. I lotion-ed the front of her leg down to her ankle. The back of her leg down to her ankle, her stomach, her back, her breast and her neck. She sat on the bed and I lotion-ed her feet.

I then tossed the lotion bottle to the side. And hovered over her. I wasn't really aroused when she came in, but our little shower just made me attracted to her big time. She went to touched me and I held her wrist. I kissed her, I kissed, licked and sucked all over her top part of her body with her wrist tightly gripped. I went as far down as my arms would allow. I came back up and rested my torso in between her legs and tasted her breast in my mouth. Felt her nipples harden in my mouth once they were hardened, I ran them over my lips like they were my chapstick, I was hoping she was nipple sensitive. I had gotten hungry, and she looked like my plate that had been fixed. I softy bit her, giving her small whelps. I turned her over and put her in the doggy style position and ate her pussy from the back, then I slid my fingers inside of her tight little pussy and started pushing them in with my hips and finger fucked her doggy style. I slide my fingers out and tried to slide my clit on hers. I wanted to feel her pussy hole on my clit, I wanted her to squeeze her pussy on my clit, if only on the rim, I was hunching her pussy hole, I took her hips and banged her heart shaped ass against my crotch. We were both dripping wet. I just didn't know if she was good or if she wanted more. I laid her flat and opened her legs with mine and rubbed her clit until she began squirming, it was so hard on my fingers, it just made me want to put it in my mouth. I turned her over, put her legs over my shoulders and licked her clit, tossed my tongue in her pussy and tried to stretch her a little, pulling on the rim with my curled tongue, I'd finally got an "oh" out of her. I put my finger back in and then climbed up her body and put her nipple back in my mouth. I got really excited her and my knuckles were banging the shit out that tight lil' pussy. I finger fucked her for like two minutes, then I instructed her to sit on my face and fucked my face 'til she came, and she did just that. She grabbed the head board and started bucking on my face. She'd found a nice rhythm. While she got excited, I started jacking my clit off and right after she stated to come, I came. She slid off my face and kissed my mouth, that mouth nice. I chuckled and smiled. She bent down and whispered in my ear.

"I want some."

My smile went away immediately. I had this crazy fetish. I love fems up in me but on they niguh side. It's a twisted warped fetish in some ways. I whispered back in a questionable voice,

"You want some? Why?"

"Cause, I know it's tight?"

This dumb bitch (my pussy) gone jump, so, I chuckled. And I said

"She said, that sounds like game."

"Oh, that's what she said, let me talk to her then."

She slid her fingers down my body and in-between my legs. Felt my clit and slid her fingers inside.

"Oh, she was almost relaxed now, you tensing up again."

I just laid there. I wanted to give her me, but just couldn't. I chuckled, she'd need to just explore on her own and get what she wanted out of me.

I'm going to go put it on our energies, they had changed in the matter of minutes. I wasn't sure had she did this before, if she wanted to do this. I was thinking of every possible way to get out of this situation. As she walked back in the room my phone had rung and I started towards it, she grabbed it, looked at it and tossed it,

"it's not your peoples, you good, you busy."

"Nah, I need to look see who it was."

She started harnessing up and I looked at the phone. She smacked my ass as I walked to the chair,

"Really Sig?

"Yea really."

"Oh, wow."

I'd enjoyed it, but I just didn't know if I was ready to enjoy some thing I wanted. I looked at the phone and was disappointed that it wasn't important.

"I told you, it wasn't your peoples."

"I know."

"Come here, help me with this."

"Sig what's this shii."

I started to help buckle and stopped and asked,

What's up with this?

"What's up with what PC? She pinched my nipple.

"I can't have none?"

She asked,

"Baby, I ain't say that."

"Then help me with this."

"You did this before?"

"What you think?"

"To be honest, I have no clue."

"If I want some, do you think I did this before?"

"Well shii, imma hope I'm special enough that you'd just want some."

"You are."

She nipped my chin like I was a little bitch and said,

"Nah, I did this before."

She laid on the bed after strapping up. Handed me a bag and said go get pretty.

"I beg your pardon."

"Baby can yo got put that on?" she stroked her strap.

started jacking my clit off and right after she stated to come, I came. She slid off my face and kissed my mouth, that mouth nice. I chuckled and smiled. She bent down and whispered in my ear.

"I want some."

My smile went away immediately. I had this crazy fetish. I love fems up in me but on they niguh side. It's a twisted warped fetish in some ways. I whispered back in a questionable voice,

"You want some? Why?"

"Cause, I know it's tight?"

This dumb bitch (my pussy) gone jump, so, I chuckled. And I said

"She said, that sounds like game."

"Oh, that's what she said, let me talk to her then."

She slid her fingers down my body and in-between my legs. Felt my clit and slid her fingers inside.

"Oh, she was almost relaxed now, you tensing up again."

I just laid there. I wanted to give her me, but just couldn't. I chuckled, she'd need to just explore on her own and get what she wanted out of me.

I'm going to go put it on our energies, they had changed in the matter of minutes. I wasn't sure had she did this before, if she wanted to do this. I was thinking of every possible way to get out of this situation. As she walked back in the room my phone had rung and I started towards it, she grabbed it, looked at it and tossed it,

"it's not your peoples, you good, you busy."

"Nah, I need to look see who it was."

She started harnessing up and I looked at the phone. She smacked my ass as I walked to the chair,

"Really Sig?

"Yea really."

"Oh, wow."

I'd enjoyed it, but I just didn't know if I was ready to enjoy some thing I wanted. I looked at the phone and was disappointed that it wasn't important.

"I told you, it wasn't your peoples."

"I know."

"Come here, help me with this."

"Sig what's this shii."

I started to help buckle and stopped and asked,

What's up with this?

"What's up with what PC? She pinched my nipple.

"I can't have none?"

She asked,

"Baby, I ain't say that."

"Then help me with this."

"You did this before?"

"What you think?"

"To be honest, I have no clue."

"If I want some, do you think I did this before?"

"Well shii, imma hope I'm special enough that you'd just want some."

"You are."

She nipped my chin like I was a little bitch and said,

"Nah, I did this before."

She laid on the bed after strapping up. Handed me a bag and said go get pretty.

"I beg your pardon."

"Baby can yo got put that on?" she stroked her strap.

I lowered my head. I really didn't know my feelings. I was very attracted to her. Bottoming out was just so mental for me. And I have no clue why. I pout-ily walked to the bathroom dragging the bag. With a lower head.

"Baby", she said.

I didn't turn around.

She said "baby",

"Oh ok, that's about to change."

I closed the bathroom door and locked it.

I opened the bag and it was feminine type under wear with stockings and boots. When I was younger I guess I was a tad insecure. But it was a wrap after the first time I seen that I was cute. So sometimes insecurities with looks crept into my sub conscious but not really. Getting laid was never a problem. But, I don't know the concept of pussy and keeping some one. And having good pussy or giving to someone deserving of you always just crept. But, I put the underwear and matching bra on, it was a yellow color that went with my skin tone very nicely. Lightly moisturized my locks and braided them. A confident hairstyle I had, was my two braids.

I don't know if she really knew what she was asking for, or I didn't know what she was really asking. I put moisturizer on my lips and moisturized my face. And went out the door after putting on some scents.

I walked out,

"Yeah babe! Look at you, all sexy and shii."

I just looked.

"Baby, come here."

I don't know, I was just resisting. I knew how I got probably. She taps the bed for me to come to the bed.

"Can you come here please."

I walked over and stood there and grabbed my hands.

"You look pretty."

I ignored her. She found my line of vision with hers. And looked at me and said,

"Babe, you look pretty."

And she softly squeezed my hands.

I softly said,

"thank you."

"Is this what it takes for me to get some pussy? She said.

That was a weird question but seemed like an appropriate one.

"Why do you want some pussy, I think my question may be?

"Oh."

"I wanna feel you cum, while I'm inside of you." She said.

"Is that reason enough?"

I was a little lost with a response. She rubbed my arm with her hand.

"You look pretty babe. The yellow with your complexion is beautiful."

I softly said,

"thank you."

She took the rubber bands off the ends of my braids and un braided my two braids. She laid my hair on my shoulders.

"Your hair is getting long babe. Can I make you cum?

"If you want to."

"I want to."

"You're funny babe."

"Why you say that?"

"Can I kiss you on your neck?"

"You don't have to ask."

"Oh, you giving yourself to me?" she said.

"I don't know how to do that. Do you deserve me. What you gone do with me after I give

myself to you."

"I'll show you all that."

"What's your favorite line? Can I have some?"

She rubbed my arms and my nipples became erected. She noticed it and began rubbing it

with her thumb. It was actually driving me bonkers. She was kissing my neck and rubbing my

nipple with her thumb.

"You want some pussy?"

I whispered in her ear as a question.

"No, I want some of you."

She was saying some acceptable answers to some things. I don't think I ever knew how much a

mind game I was sexually. She slid her hand down from my harden nipple to my throbbing clit.

And her mouth found its way from my neck to my mouth. She took my hand and put it on her strap.

I looked quizzical,

"You want me to dyck you down don't you?"

"I don't know, I don't know if you know how to do it right.

"I slang this", she said.

I chuckled because she was so feminine. Which was a good thing but there was a dynamic to it that

needed to be investigated first.

"Oh ok, well this here is deep. And tight."

"Oh ok, well, I'm about to be snug up in it deep then."

"Mmmm, I responded."

"Oh, you want me with my legs open?"

She finished my sentence with,

"and that pussy wet."

I stroked her strapped how I needed to be stroke, she started she started air stroking catching them rhythm?

"And, questioned, yeah?"

I said, "yeah."

She rubbed my clit so nice. She slid her fingers in.

"Oh my God, you're throbbing so hard, baby you need me in there don't you?"

I lowered my head and puffed and exhale. I grabbed her face and started back kissing her. I took her fingers and put them on the knot that was inside my vagina. It was so hard it was suppose to be.

"Baby rub it."

"Yeah?"

"Yeah."

She rubbed it and I kissed her and moaned. She felt so nice inside me. My kisses were so slow and passionate, I could barely continue. I just wanted to enjoy her fingers inside me. She laid me back on the bed.

"Oh, I'm 'bout to make this pussy buss."

I chuckled and said,

"well you'll be the first."

"What?"

"You'll be the first."

"Bust how? From being inside me with this?" as I tugged on her strap.

"Yeah."

"Oh yeah, you'll be the first."

"Oh well, yeah I'm about to make that happen."

BIZ CLASS

Hated night classes, nah let me stop bitchin' completely happy I was accepted to the program, classes happened so fast, still need to get situated. A car had pulled in next to me, some jawn in the mirror messing with her hair before she put the car in park. But I don't know, wasn't too much of my business. Inhaled my el on last time type deep. Held the smoke until I got out the car. Closed the door blew the smoke and hit the alarm. And headed to class.

Night classes, I was such a morning person. I walked to class open the door, and the professor asked "business or tech" major. Tech, business, double major. Ok sit there. Ok, so this class is for 18 months, in this class you will have a business partner and start a business from scratch. Pick a partner or pick the person next to you. Every one basically picked the person that was sitting next to them, some of them knew one another, and I imagine the others it was the easiest thing to do. I was sitting alone. When the teacher came over and said,

"Oh, you are going to be a single duckling huh?"

Just then the girl who was in her mirror in the parking lot walked in.

"Oh ok, Ms. Tardy and single duckling. You, you sit there." The professor said.

She flashed a smile put down some purse and smiled at me, she knew I was faded as fuch, so she didn't bother much. I just slowly turned.

"Ok, again as I said before we paired up 18-month class and about 35 % of your masters degree. Good luck, if one of you are in class, then the both of you are in class. If one of you fails, both of you fail."

"Oh, we don't fail over." Hear my partner said.

I chuckled. I shook my head.

"You have the rest of this class to pick a business and then you are dismissed. I suggest you take the allowed time to really discuss what strengths and weaknesses you have and pick a business." Class is over at 10 pm and I am here until 11 pm each and every class. Please submit your business ideas, by 10 pm. Your business must make ten thousand dollars and the funding will go to your departments of the school and any other department of the school you'd like to help fund. Are there any questions?"

No one said anything.

"Good."

Take a syllabus before you leave for the night and sign the attendance sheet. And sign the attendance sheet with your name for your partner when there's just one of you.

I sat there, waiting for shawtie to say something.

"Is there a mall or something down the street can we go get something to eat and talk about this?"

"Um, I have no idea. I'm not from around here."

"Ok, just follow me ok?"

"Ok."

I guess she really remembered that I parked next to her. We got to our cars and she seen my plates and said,

"Oh, you really not from here."

I chuckled and said,

"Nah I'm not…"

She got in her car and pulled out, she waited at the end of the drive way for me, I was behind her shortly. We drove about ten minutes and found some food places that were in the same area. We pulled side by side and she said which one, I pointed to tacos. And we parked close to the taco building.

We parked and got out of our cars walked up to the taco place, I grabbed the door for her, she smiled. I shook my head. We got in line there was a little line.

"Well I guess, I'll introduce myself because I guess you aren't."

I looked confused and shook my head.

"My name or well they call me Pose. Oh ok, Pose. Hi Pose, they call me Codie. Ok Codie, she shook her head. She was next in line and I wanted to go blow again. But she ordered. And then I ordered.

She said she was going to the bathroom and could I listen out for the order. I was salt because I was going to go smoke. I still went out the front and smoked. And listened for the orders. It took about 5 minutes for our food.

They called our numbers and I grabbed the trays and she came out shortly.

"So, Codie, what type of business are we going to run for the next 18 months. I arrogantly said,

"It doesn't matter to me. Are you one of those slacker type of students?

"Nawhl, I just think that we can be successful at what ever we do. That is all."

"Oh, ok, ok, cool."

"So, what are you in to?

"Me? Um, computers, sports."

"Ok, so I like make up and hair and fashion.

"Um food or fashion?

"Oh yeah, food would make sense since we ended up at some where to eat. But, I rather go

with fashion."

"Ok, I'm wit it.

"Ok, cool.

"Fashion. Ok, so we have to think of stuff."

We talked for about 2 and half hours, we mapped out a lot of stuff too. And, planned most of

the 18 months out. It was interesting we followed the schedule of the syllabus as well. After we did

that, she asked,

"Do you need me to go back and fill the paper or can you."

I said,

"I can."

We parted ways.

"See you next class."

"Aiyte, cool be good."

I had some shit to do, I was looking for a spot, just moved down here, had a bunch of shit to figure

out. I don't know why I am always starting school when shit be so hectic. But 3 more degrees and

we good, well 4 and some certs, but it is what it is… "die trying."

I rode back to school, put down that we were going to have a fashion business and headed for

the motel 6. I was suppose to go see an apartment in two days. Actually, right before the next class.

Went back to the motel and called it a night. My next two days weren't bad, but the food was a bit different, I wasn't finding all the brands that I was use to and had to trust picking something out.

I walked in to class and sat next to my partner. And she said,

"Girl I didn't get your number, I wasn't even going to come in, but all we knew were nicknames and shit."

"Oh, ok. How are you?"

"I'm good."

The teacher walked in and said,

"Ok who wants to go first."

Everyone looked at one another. Go first. Oh, how many people read the syllabus. Partner and I looked at one another, we knew we read it, but didn't remember a "have next class." Everyone who had it, took out their syllabus and frantically thought of losing points.

"Everyone calm down. I just want a small explanation of what your business will consist of and whatever else you discussed or any areas you are concerned about. Ok, so, I'll randomly pic someone. Who is doing the beer business? You're up."

These two guys got up and explain their business, the class were to ask questions and he critique what they done and not done and explained the pace of business.

"Next fashion."

We stood up and explain the business, he asked for the name of the business. She looked at me and shrugged and said "Woven." He asked some specifics, some we hadn't addressed, but he said,

Good job, "single duckling" and "Ms. Tardi". We smiled and sat down. He went through the other groups and asked were there any questions.

The teacher advised us to read the assignment and that there would be a quiz next class. He also said that he was very strong on vocabulary and suggest being very familiar with it. He also said that class wasn't until next week. And that we needed to have part of our business plan put together. He dismissed class, once class was dismissed Pose said,

"When would you like to meet up? Oh, it's up to you, any time is cool.

"Ok, how about Saturday afternoon."

"Sure."

"Hey I heard there was a morning class."

"Yeah there is, they meet twice a week, instead of three times."

"Oh, ok."

"What, you thinking about changing?"

"Yeah, I kinda don't like night classes."

"Oh, you can't leave sweetie. We already picked a business."

"Yeah, I can, you have 10 days to drop and add."

"Oh no, not in this class. Once you pick your partners. He do not give incompletes."

"Oh no, I didn't know that, ok. I just really hate night classes. I'm such a morning person."

It was Wednesday and we were going to meet up Saturday. That gave me a few days to get some things done. Needed to do a lot of running around and had no clue as to where anything really was.

Not sure who I was mad at in life. They say you're suppose to take responsibility. But I'm not sure all this rests on me. But I should have definitely been doing this twenty years ago. But so be it.

I went about my way for the next few days. Got a text Friday night.

"Are we still on for tomorrow? We are we meeting up? It was Pose.

"Hey, um sure, definitely, doesn't matter. Ok I'll come to you. Oh ok, well I just moved in,
I   don't have much."

Thank goodness the couch was delivered today.

"Oh, it doesn't matter, you have internet right?

"Yes."

"Ok, well to get some work done, that's pretty much all we need, see you tomorrow."

"Ok."

"Cool."

I studied for the rest of the night. It was 11:30 the next day, and I got a call.

"We truly need to plan better. We had no time, I don't have an address."

"Oh, ok."

She seemed a little snappy. But she was right. In business failing to plan is definitely planning to
fail.

She got to the spot about 15 minutes later. She was dressed just to study. I guess I felt like
my crib was a little under dressed.

She came in and asked,

"can I take off my shoes."

I was wondering why she was wearing shoes.

"Give me like 5 minutes and we can get started."

"Sure." I asked, "do you mind if I smoke.

"She said, "nah."

So I rolled an el while she was doing what ever she was doing I really don't know on the phone I

gathered. I gathered the materials to study and plan. And we sat at the table and began brainstorming and discussing topics. She said we would have a fashion show in 3 months and we will have raised our 10k. Here I was, that was my major concern. I'd become such an introvert, my people skills had definitely taken the hit for them. I told her I could take care of any of the technical stuff. She said she could take care of all of the models and designers. So it was a go. But the fashion show wasn't a clothing line so we needed to know what we were actually going to do.

DOCUMENT 57

"Can I have some sour patch kids and some lemon heads?"

"You might as well get some m&ms with peanuts and some gummi bears."

"Nah, I just want my sour patch kids and some lemon heads."

"Oh ok, my fault."

"Nahwl, you good."

"Oh, ok."

She left towards the door.

"Can I get two entourages please.

I walked out. I started walking to the studio. A black Maserati pulled to the stop sign as I crossed the street.

"Um can we hurry this up please.

I looked it was the girl getting the candy from the store. I purposely dropped my lighter and slowly picked it up.

She flicked her high beams.

And I asked,

"Really though."

"So, I'm saying, can I call you though?"

"To say what?"

"Good morning."

"Cute."

"Oh, so, you think I'm cute?"

"This your dude car though?"

"Scratch that."

"Oh ok. I guess, I think I can grab that."

"So, I'm saying, can I call you though?"

"Give me your number and I'll send you my number in a few."

"Awl here you go."

"Nah, I am serious."

I punched my number in, locked the number in,

"I'm saying, imma just hit send now, and see how quick that was."

She chuckled and shook her head. I backed up and ushered my arm for her to pull off. She pulled off.

"Be good."

"I'm great."

I just smiled and shook my head wasn't sure if she was quick with it or needed the last word.

Headed back to the studio.

"Hey babe, you know you left the lights on."

"I didn't leave my lights on."

She grabbed the key and pushed a few buttons and her lights didn't go off.

"Oh, my goodness that is going to drain my battery."

She chuckled to herself remembering she flashed her beams and thought that it was ironic that they were stuck.

She dropped some chicken fingers and called Maserati.

"Maserati?"

"Hey, yes, can I speak to the maintenance department?"

"Um, how can I help you?"

"Well my lights are on and won't turn off."

"Oh ok, there was a patch update for the radio system. And, it may or may not leave the light on after it ran its course depending on the model. Push the window button three times and then the lock. And they will cut off. Do you need me to hold while you do that?"

"No, window three times and the lock."

"Car on or off?"

"With the car turned off ma'am."

"Ok, thank you."

She scurried out to the car and tapped the window button then the lock button and the lights went off. She checked them to see if they worked and scurried back in to the kitchen, which was a medium size restaurant.

She put the keys back in her purse and washed her hands and took up the chicken fingers. She finished making the order for the customer. She bagged up the food and gave the customer their food and she took her phone out her back pocket and looked through the phone for last call out. It popped up.

"You broke my lights", she texted the number.

I didn't see the text until a few hours later, my phone wasn't close to me. I was in the studio working on some designs when my phone rang.

"Hello."

"Hello."

"Who's this?"

"I thought you saved my number."

"No, I saved my number in your phone. I chuckled... what's up with you?"

"You broke my car."

"Nawhl, not me. I can't afford that jawn."

"My lights got stuck."

I began laughing.

"Oh nawhl, that's not my fault though…"

"Yes, it is."

"Oh ok. I got you on a cup of coffee."

"Oh ok, I will hold you to that."

"No doubt."

"Ok, you have a good day."

"You too."

Got back to some editing for a few more hours grabbed some sleep. I got up at 7, I texted shawtie around 9.

"Good morning."

"Good morning." She responded.

"Have a good day."

"You too."

I had some running around to do, things were really getting busy, wasn't exactly where I thought I needed to be but slow progress better than no progress. I was headed to the gym when I got a text.

"Can I get that coffee you owe me?"

"Sure. Where are you?"

"You know the beauty salon on the west side, near the pool hall?"

"Yeah, the green and black building."

"Yea."

"Sure, give me like 20 minutes."

"Ok."

Headed in that direction and grabbed her a coffee and a French toast platter, she was under the dryer when I got there. Handed her the food and the coffee,

"Aw you got me food that was sweet of you. What you up to?"

"Headed to the gym."

"Oh, ok."

"I'll call or text you later."

She stated it with a soft quizzical tone.

I said, "ok." And left.

I hit the gym then headed back to the studio, I needed to head to the meeting with the artist. On my way out shawtie called me,

"What you up to?"

"Headed to a meeting."

"Oh, you aren't close."

"No, not really, I can call you when I get back though."

"Yeah that'll work."

"Aiyte."

Went to the meeting and turned out pretty well ended up signing the artist.

I was excited about the growth we were making. Headed back around the way. Hit shawtie up.

"I'm around the way."

My phone rang.

"Yo."

"Hey."

"How are you?"

"Good."

"My lights got stuck."

I began laughing.

"Oh nawhl, that's not my fault though…"

"Yes, it is."

"Oh ok. I got you on a cup of coffee."

"Oh ok, I will hold you to that."

"No doubt."

"Ok, you have a good day."

"You too."

Got back to some editing for a few more hours grabbed some sleep. I got up at 7, I texted shawtie around 9.

"Good morning."

"Good morning." She responded.

"Have a good day."

"You too."

I had some running around to do, things were really getting busy, wasn't exactly where I thought I needed to be but slow progress better than no progress. I was headed to the gym when I got a text.

"Can I get that coffee you owe me?"

"Sure. Where are you?"

"You know the beauty salon on the west side, near the pool hall?"

"Yeah, the green and black building."

"Yea."

"Sure, give me like 20 minutes."

"Ok."

Headed in that direction and grabbed her a coffee and a French toast platter, she was under the dryer when I got there. Handed her the food and the coffee,

"Aw you got me food that was sweet of you. What you up to?"

"Headed to the gym."

"Oh, ok."

"I'll call or text you later."

She stated it with a soft quizzical tone.

I said, "ok." And left.

I hit the gym then headed back to the studio, I needed to head to the meeting with the artist. On my way out shawtie called me,

"What you up to?"

"Headed to a meeting."

"Oh, you aren't close."

"No, not really, I can call you when I get back though."

"Yeah that'll work."

"Aiyte."

Went to the meeting and turned out pretty well ended up signing the artist.

I was excited about the growth we were making. Headed back around the way. Hit shawtie up.

"I'm around the way."

My phone rang.

"Yo."

"Hey."

"How are you?"

"Good."

"That's good, what's up?"

"Nothing, what you up to?"

"Nothing, just getting back around the way."

"Oh, ok."

"Did you wanna do something?"

"I guess, I wouldn't mind?"

"Movies, pool?"

"Movies is good."

"Ok, cinema-plex in a hour?"

"Yeah, that'll work.

"Ok."

I showered and headed to the theatre. I got there a few minutes before she did. I see her pull

up.

Where you at? I got a text.

"Near the door."

"Oh ok."

She looked and seen me grabbed her things and walked up to the door, I opened the door.

"Popcorn."

"Yeah."

We ordered our snacks and headed to the theatre. Movies was good, I definitely was trying not to be

a talker during the movie. The movie was a pretty good movie. I always like tech conspiracy

movies. She said,

I liked it but I didn't all the way understand the movie.

After the movie, I needed to use the restroom, so we went towards the line that was slowly growing and we discussed the movie a little bit. I finally got to use the bathroom. She decided she needed to go as well. Washed our hands and headed to the parking lot. I walked her to the car she asked me what was about to do.

I told her,

I am about to go grab a tea while I waited for the next train … "where you stay?" she asked.

"I can take you."

"Studio on the south west side, no I can wait."

"Get in the car" she said slightly demanding. We talked during the ride. And in about 20 minutes, reached the studio. I invited her in.

She looked at some of the designs that were laid out and asked.

"Can I take a closer look?"

She asked,

"What do you do?"

"Marketing and advertisement."

She said,

"Oh, some of your mock ups are interesting."

She stayed for a few and said,

I need to head home. I have to cater an even tomorrow. I need to be up early. "

She left, and I got to editing …

I woke up to a knock on the studio door.

"Delivery."

"Delivery?"

I yelled,

Nah, I ain't order nothing.

As I was saying that a text came through

      "I made you breakfast."

I opened the door and the delivery guy handed me food. I thanked him and grabbed two bucks to tip him with.

      "Thank you." I texted back and "good morning."

      "Good morning."

Spent all day designing some advertisement materials.

      "Mind coming to see me?" I received a text.

      Replied, "ummm sure, no problem. Give me about a hour and a half."

      "Yeah, that's fine."

Had to take some things across town and then head that way. She texted me the address

We sat and talked she actually ended up falling asleep in my arms. I woke up around 2 am asked her her plans for the next day.

She said,

      "my day is a normal day and rested her head back on my arms around 9 o'clock.

We both woke up, I headed to the studio. She said

      I will get up with you later if that' cool?"

Spent my day just gathering materials ready to pump some shit out had to be on go and couldn't let up off the gas this year. Had some catching up to do I guess.

Had got a call that made me extremely excited. But put extra pressure on me but pressure I willingly accepted.

I got a text from shawtie, she asked,

      "What are you up to?"

      "I'm late running some errands. Usually daily stuff."

      "I enjoyed last night."

"Last night?"

"Yea, just talking and chilling not many do that these days."

"Oh ok, cool. I got some brownie points."

"Oh, you racking up points."

"Of course, how many I need?"

"I'll let you know."

"Oh goodness, don't be getting me for my points."

"I won't."

"What you up to though?"

"Not much."

We'd been talking about a month and a half and hadn't been intimate just yet. It wasn't too much on my mind but I was definitely extremely attracted to her. And I'd dated quite a few women who liked a more aggressive lover. But the time just never seemed right.

She texted me I was in the editing bay.

"Hey love, how are you?"

"I'm good what's up?"

"Are you busy?"

"At the moment, yes, but in about 40 mins no, what's up?"

Can you take my car to get washed, I forgot and I have an event at the end of the work day and have no time to get it done myself.

"Um sure."

Finished up what I needed to get done and headed to her restaurant. She had one of the best restaurants in town. Definitely was booming and the food was good. When I got there, she had my cheese and macaroni and chocolate cake. She kept me fed. I appreciated that. I grabbed her keys and took her car to get detailed. Took me about a hour and half and brought her car back. And

headed back to the studio. I feel asleep when my phone rang about two hours later.

"You were sleep?"

As I picked up the phone

"Yeah."

"Come over, or I can come over."

"I'll come over."

Through some sweats on and went over to her house. Rang the bell. Took my jacket and

shoes off and crashed on the couch.

"You gone go to sleep?"

"Uh yeah that's what I was doing."

She did a stomp pouty thing. I chuckled

"Well at least come up stairs and get in the bed."

We'd fell asleep together a few times so I thought nothing of it this time. We got to the bed room and

I climbed across to the un-dented side of the mattress. She laid down and watched tv.

"Do you find me attractive?"

A question came from nowhere.

I chuckled. "What?"

"Do you find me attractive? You've never hit on me.

"Yes, I think that you are very attractive, hence me attempting to show you massive respect."

She flips over with a smile,

"oh, so you just trying to respect me …"

"Yeah."

"Oh, that's cute."

"But you don't have to respect me, well I want you to respect me, but damn you can at least

try and steal a hug or something occasionally."

See that's the thing, I'd want to steal more than a hug.

Are we really going to have this conversation while lying in the bed though?"

"I'm going to sleep."

I slid off my sweats and fell off to sleep.

I woke up about 2 she snuggled up close to me and I looked at her face as she slept. I don't know what made me do it, but I began kissing her lips. They were so soft and warm I actually just wanted to suck on them for a while, but she began kissing me back.

She pulled back and said you're not going to gargle or nothing. I pulled back, she pulled me back towards her and began kissing me back. I slid my hand along her thigh and to her ass and rubbed her booty. She was thick in all the right places and I started to feel her heat beat rise. I grabbed her ass and slid my hand up her shirt to her breast. I softly pinched her nipple and ran my hand over it as it hardened. I ducked under the covers to kiss on her stomach and slid her panties off. I positioned my torso in-between her legs. I softly bit her thighs on the inside and squeezed them squeezes them firmly and opened her legs to expose her vagina. It looked a little engorged…. I placed my mouth over her vagina lips and her clitoris slowly curled my tongue and clipped her vagina hole and began massaging the base of her clit with my tongue. Slowly. It kept getting harder and hard. I tongue kissed her vagina as I heard moans of pleasure she grabbed my head and thrust her hips she grind-ed her hips I was getting so turned on, she grabbed the back of my head and smashed me closed to her pussy. And grind-ed, her clit vein was so hard my tongue was rubbing it softly slowly but firm. I firmly put my lips on her clit and licked the tip of clit with my tongue …….

THIS IS RARE

Second Annual Bastian Urban Haute Couture. Read the banner, I couldn't believe that I got

invited to this, and so soon. Wasn't too hype about my designs, but never the less, I was here

because my stitch says I'm that bitch. My friend actually got the security for the event but we

wouldn't see much of one another. I was in the summer casual line up. And had about an hour to

until we were going to check in. Since I was going to be here all night, I just grabbed a room at the

hotel on the same block, but not same as the event.

I walked through the hotel vestibule to the elevator. Someone came and stood next to me,

and the elevator was coming up from the garage. The doors opened my stomach dropped, we hadn't

really dealt with one another for about 3 months, I actually tried to stay out her way, avoid not be

nowhere near whatever she was doing. The person that stood next to me made a gesture as to ask

was I getting on the elevator. I stepped on the elevator, she said,

"Hello."

I exhaled through my nose and said,

"Hello."

This elevator was going to be long,

"Can we talk?"

"There's no need."

"Don't be like that."

"Please, you know I have a temper, please let's not do this. I'm busy til ten."

"And, Lord knows you go to bed early."

"Yes."

"Please can we talk?"

"Room 1006, I should be back by eleven."

"Ok."

I got off at the tenth floor. She remained on the elevator.

"Talk to you later." she blurted out, in a where are your manners voice.

"See you later."

I really couldn't get unfocused right now, needed to pull this show off. Changed my clothes and then headed to the models to make sure everything was ok with them.

.

The show was good and I made connects with vendors, it was definitely a good show. Wrapped up and headed back to my room, it was 10:44. I actually just laid on the couch and nodded off until I heard a knock at the door. I got up and answered the door. It was her.

"Hello."

"Hello, how are you?"

"Making it."

"Making it, you stay making it."

"Please, don't even start."

"You right."

"What do you want to talk about?"

"Us."

"Us, there is no us."

"I know, why is that? Why do you have to be like this?"

"What yo? Is this the conversation you're really trying to have?"

"I miss you."

"Don't do that."

"I do."

"You good, you'll be alright."

"You don't miss me."

"Yo, why, why are we having this conversation."

The phone rang.

"Babe, I left my gun in the truck, can you bring it to me." a male voice said.

"Ok babe, I'll be there in like twenty minutes."

"Ok, we aren't done until five."

"Ok. I'm finished, everything went great."

"Awesome, see, and you didn't want to do the sewing thing."

"I know, I'm one my way."

"Ok."

I hung up phone.

"Oh, that's you?"

"What? I scowled and asked. Well, it was nice talking to you."

"We not finished talking. I'll be here when you get back."

"You in the way right now."

"Oh, that's how you talk to me."

"Look kinda got you out of my system, I don't mean no harm or nothing, just self peace, ma ma."

"Ok, well I'll be here when you get back."

Grabbed the keys to his truck and went to the parking lot. Got to my car to drive to his car to take his fire arm to him. Drove to him and gave him his gun. Dreaded going back to the hotel. But headed back to the hotel. Got back to the hotel room in about an hour.

She'd taken her clothes off and had on this matching camisole type of under garment. She still looked fantastic.

"What are you doing?" She stepped up to me and ran her hand underneath my tee shirt.

"What do you mean, what am I doing?"

"I told you I missed you and seem like you have time your peoples aren't coming home til 5."

I moved her hands.

"First of all, he isn't coming here. But that's neither here nor or there."

"What are you doing?"

"Can you put your clothes on?"

"I don't look good?"

"I didn't say this, but I can't do this and you know I can't do this."

"Why?"

"Why you trying to drive me crazy?"

"I'm not."

"So, why, why are you here, why?"

"Look, do you want to talk about this or not?"

I looked angrily to each direction east and west and said,

"No, I never wanted to talk about it, you made your decision. So, there's no conversation needed. Please, you know I don't like to curse at women and you're getting me there."

She grabbed my hands,

"Please don't be like that. I need you not to be like this."

"Look I don't know how to be, like this I feel how I feel. I can't change my feelings and do not desire to change them."

"I have some things to do, was there anything else you wanted."

"You, you of all people are going to leave me like this? When I told you, I missed you."
She walked up close to me.

"I don't think it's a coincidence that we ran in to one another. You always said if I needed you just think about you and we will be one in rhythm. And I've been thinking about you."

"I'm sorry, but I don't want you to ask me to be be sorry."

"Did I ask for a fucking apology? Did I, I didn't even ask for this fucking conversation."

"Why are you so upset?"

"The fuck yo, please."

"Can you touch me, please?"

"Nawhl, you have some one that touches you, you don't need me to touch you."

"You act like, you not talking to someone."

"Yo, what else do you want."

"Please, can you touch me the way you do?"

"I don't touch you and I haven't touched you."
She took my hand and put it down the middle of her chest. She closed her eyes and enjoyed her hand guiding my hand to touch her.

"You're so warm still."
She took my hand and made two of my fingertips run across her collar bone.

"You didn't miss me? You don't think about me anymore?"
She took her hand and pinched my nipple. I took a long blink.

"Please stop."

"I don't want to though. I need you right now. Is he going to get mad?"

"Nah, we not together, just friends."

"Yawl not fucking?"

She slid her hands down my sweats.

"Yawl fucking, 'cause you got on panties."

I took her hand off my ass and out of my pants.

"I don't want to do this."

"But, will you?"

I closed my eyes and looked away. She took my hand and put it in her pants.

"See how hard and wet you got me? "You tight?"

She looked at me and knew I was hurt. She grabbed my face and kissed me, a tear ran down my cheek she held my face and kissed me.

"I know, but I need you right now though, doesn't that mean anything?"

It didn't not at all. Another tear dropped and I shook my head, "no."

She pushed my fingers inside of her. I know you feel it. I did, her heart beat. Her heartbeat was beating strong and aggressively and I felt it through her throbbing vagina.

"You still get me like that. Kiss me."

Her clit jumped as my finger glazed over it, I knew I couldn't leave her like that, but I still, I still didn't want to make love to her. I kissed her back.

Softly explaining how hurt I was with every tongue and lip interaction, I hadn't felt her in so long, hadn't felt a woman in a minute either. This was the last thing I needed right now. She stuck her hands in my panties, her fingers slid in with more ease than usual. She looked at me, I lowered my head in shame she went for my spot and grabbed my face kind of firm by my cheeks as a tear dropped from her face. She began to kiss me hard she softly rubbed my spot.

She said … "but I missed you though."

We went to the couch in the living room section of the hotel suite. Then went to the bedroom before sitting down. There was no need to go to the couch.

She started kissing my neck, I picked her up and wrapped her legs around my waste and sat on the bed. She was sucking on my earlobe softly. Nibbling on my ear like a very neat girl eating a candy apple. Making sure not to mess up her teeth, nor her lip stick.

She started taking the rubber band tie out of my hair and rub my head and hair. She began grinding. I turned her around and over. And laid her on her back, I took my sweats off, she chuckled.

"Oh panties, panties they are cute. I better not leave my laundry next to yours."

I side eyed here like for real we really had jokes.

"No baby, you look cute. Pretty sure who ever he is …"

"Leave it be please."

She snapped the thick band to my panties as I climbed on top of her. I forced my leg in-between her legs to open her legs.

I lifted up the lace camisole, I took a minute because I hadn't seen her in a minute. But then I went in to the thought of her being someone else's, so I needed to just fade off. I firmly bit her neck and bit her nipples before enjoying her nipples hardening in my mouth. I grabbed them with my hand and squeezed them. I heard a moan from her which turned me on extremely, it let me know she still enjoyed my touch. I thought about her being with someone else and laid my head on her naked chest a tear came from my eye down her chest down to the side of her breast. I wiped my eyes on her chest. And kissed her neck. I needed to get through this, so I just was going to enjoy the moment as best I could, I definitely had to take a different angle to get through this. It wasn't she wasn't still beautiful. Just that someone else had been with her that I couldn't get out of my mind. I mean I knew, I always thought that some people aren't made for one person. Some people never find one person. Perhaps it was because I wasn't enough. I really don't know but it, I don't… as I got lost in my thoughts.

I licked down the middle of her chest to her belly button. She grabbed one of my breast and started squeezing it, she was touching more than shed ever had, not that she never, but she wasn't really ever this attentive. It through me for a moment. I went back to her breast and sucked on them as if I'd never see them again, and that they'd always remember me. She began squiring she rubbed in between my legs.

"Daddi, I missed you."

"I don't have my strap."

"You don't need it, you know what how to treat her, you know how to take care of her." My nipples harden at her saying that. I came up and kissed her neck then kissed her deep in her mouth. She wrapped her arms around me as I kissed her. I went back in to a push up position and slid my way down. I removed her panties and opened her legs. Although someone else had been trying to talk to her she still looked pretty. I spit on her and smeared my spit on her pussy. I opened her pussy lips and put my mouth on her hardened clit, she let out a heavy sigh of pleasure. And a,

"shit."

shortly after "fuck" followed.

"Baby, you feel so damn good."

I melted at those words I know she felt the tears. As I started passionately sucking on her clit and her pussy.

"Baby?"

She always wanted to talk to me when my mouth was full, guess some things didn't change. Started licking her clit and kissing it softly as I slid my fingers in her pussy firmly initially put two in there then jammed three inside of her, and said,

"Oh, I guess you need three or more now."

"I just need you in me deep baby."

I started aggressively fucking her with my fingers, she knew it was from hurt and anger. She apologized while enjoying how I was fucking her.

"Baby I'm sorry, fuck ..."

I put my hip thrust with my fingers to really fuck her good. My penis envy crept in my mental's. I slid my fingers out of her and got in between her legs, I opened her pussy and opened the lips to mine. I put my hard clit on hers and rubbed underneath her clit with mine while rubbing it on the rim of her pussy hole. She moaned.

"Baby what are you doing?"

I opened her legs back in to a v shaped and went put my mouth on her pussy and stuck my fingers inside her pussy, I sucked her pussy and rubbed her g spot at the same time while massaging her breast. She grabbed my head and grind her pussy in to my mouth.

"Baby, baby you feel so fucking good though. Baby?"

I know she needed the verbal cue, but I really didn't know what to say, everything I was going to say had sarcasm and hurt on it.

"This pussy trying to come for me?" I came up with.

"Yes, she wanna come for you baby. She wanna cum hard for you. She wants to leak all over you."

"Why she wanna come for me?"

"Because she missed you baby. You touch her right."

She started grinding hard I bit her thighs hard either she was going to have to wait to have sex or explain why she had bite marks on her thighs. I sucked her clit with a soft stroke and she came in my mouth.

"Shit baby."

I braced my wrist with my other hand stuck three fingers in her pussy made sure they were as wide as possible, strong as possible and fucked her pussy hole. She opened her legs, she opened to let me get deep, her pussy gets extremely wet, she was leaking on my fingers.

"Fuck", as she came again.

"Baby why you fucking me like this?"

She grabbed my wrist and held me while I fucked her pussy. I slide my fingers out and spit on her pussy again.

"Really?" she said.

I rolled over. Closed my eyes, things were awkward, wonder was she leaving, I really didn't even know why she was in town as I finished I felt the covers pull back off of me, and her on top of my legs she secured my knees she knew I was sensitive about my knees. She popped the band to my panties.

"Panties though?"

I half faced mean mugged her, and told her,

"I'm good."

"What?"

"I'm good."

"I want some though."

"Nawhl, I'm cool."

"Can I have some please?"

She stuck her finger inside me careful with her long ass nails. And rubbed my spot that swells… she felt so good inside me, I sighed at being please.

"Can I have some?"

She went down she put spit on her hand as she looked at me and smeared it on my pussy. Then put her mouth on my hard clit. She started sucking me off exposing my clit with her fingers pushing back to engulf my clit.

She got her to get so large. I ran my fingers through her hair, ending up putting a finger in her mouth she started sucking my fingers giving my fingers head. She put her finger back in and rubbed the swollen spot. I breathed heavy through my nose. Put my legs up like I was on the ob-gyn table and I reached my legs down and started squeezing her breast and softly pinching her nipples. I was about to climax and climax hard.

"You gone come for me ain't you?" she said.

I didn't say anything she rubbed the spot and looked at me.

You gone come for me aren't you. It started turning her on. She changed positions and took my hand and put me back in side of her… she took my wrist and forced my fingers into poking her pussy while she rubbed my swollen lump. She moaned in my ear. I grabbed her arm and began squeezing it to get through the climax… "fuck" as I blurted out, she went in to an attractive feminine screeching climax sound and blurted out,

"baby."

She collapsed on my chest and put her arm on me …

"I've missed you."

I just had no words.

"Please don't, just please don't."

"Ok. I guess I should go."

Yeah probably should. She got out the bed, I headed to the shower. Started the shower as she put her clothes back on.

"Really?"

"I'll wait until you get out the shower."

"If that's what you'd like to do…"

I took about a ten-minute shower and brushed my teeth. Gargled, put some panties on and an extremely tight tank top my boobs looked good.

"Can we talk?"

"No."

"But, I want to talk."

I sat on the couch and opened up my baggie of bud and started rolling.

"I'm sorry that I hurt you."

"Look I'm not hurt, have no reason to be hurt."

"But you're hurt, right?"

"Bro, I don't want to fucking talk about it."

I tilted my head to look the other way.

She said,

"Ok." bent down and kissed my forehead and said "ok."

"I said I miss you." I see a tear fall.

I fixed my hair and she headed to the door.

A CUP OF TEA

I remember checking everything on these questionnaire boxes. I couldn't believe my health was at risk like this and I may be over exaggerating a bit but perhaps I just don't pay attention in class or something, but certain things that was suppose to be common nutrition knowledge I seemed very short of, soda after soda and the worst kinds, gallons of it. Meanwhile while trying to really work on the habitual habits are hard to break.

"Diabetes, high blood pressure and the all-time favorite do you smoke cigarettes?"

"Oh, the loop hole..."

As I get down to the surgery questions, I hear my last name. I grab the clip board and being the typical meme female of collecting all of my stuff as I try to approach the rear part of the dentist office. I usually prefer to be in high end medical establishments and probably have never been in the presence of high end medial establishments. But inside of a medical building is a big no no, just archaic tools are a site that I just do not wish to really be amongst during the medical profession, unless I accidentally just committed a crime and have to be in some ones make shift surgical or whatever the patient waiting room is called while waiting to see the doctor.

I was discussing my dental history with the I imagine they are dental nurses or hygienist assistance waiting for the dentist. You'd think the common sense of dental hygiene and pain with the dentist would have clicked but no the inquisitive state of dental care still always interests me unfortunately a little too interesting.

I heard a familiar voice but really couldn't place it, but I've been on a mind my business no ear hustling path as of late, so I didn't over think it and went back to my dental checkup and consultation. My appointment lasted for about 15 more minutes. The appointment was encouraging but I was still dentally disappointed in myself.

I was getting my check out papers when I see someone who looked familiar but couldn't place her just yet. My mind started thinking, but I really wanted it to stay on path with the rest of the day and the things that I need to complete and get done off of the to do list.

I walked to the parking lot and the woman who was perplexing my memory was parked next to me, she looked as if she worked in the dental office. I was parked backed in and she was parked forward so our driver side doors were next to each other. I waited as she got situated to get in the car we both said an awkward hi, she sat down and was about to shut her door as she rolled down the window.

"You look very familiar" as I unlocked my car she says.

"I was thinking the same thing about you."

We both went through a list of possible places as I sat down in my driver side and rolled the window down and closed the door.

"Are you from like west side or ..."

"No, I'm out on this end only. Only time I was in the city was when I was young, and I went to this science program."

"At the science school." as I finished the sentence, we chuckled.

"Wow, blast from the past." I said.

We both chuckled and I guess thought back to our younger years. We discussed the program and our current fields of interest and the pandemic and everything opening back up. I needed to go grab a book at the book store.

"I was about to go get something to eat and grab a book, you want to grab a bite since we are talking about things opening."

"She said, sure."

We headed further into the county, I pulled next to her and asked her what did she want to eat. I really had no clue about food to be honest, I didn't understand this forwardness anyways really. It wasn't my style, but certain women just bring certain sides of you to surface. And at times I don't mind taking charge if someone is taking shotgun. The only thing I ever want is lasagna or a burger and we weren't really dressed to really be getting something to eat. So, I just figured we'd just eat at the closest place to the book store with an outside patio, it was a kind of nice afternoon out.

"We will just go to somewhere in the shopping center where the book store is. Do you mind If I went to the book store first?

I just didn't know what time it closed and didn't want it to close on me. We drove for a few more miles and reached the shopping center, we parked in the same manor we were parked in the dental parking lot and picked a place to eat. We got out of our cars and walked to the book store. She seemed quite interesting, perhaps book smart, as I guess I checked her out as she looked at books as I stand in the order pick up line. She still has scrubs on, so I really couldn't get a since of her style and she was some where in between the recipes and the romance novels, so, I really couldn't gather what she was really looking for in a book. As I hear my last name.

"Hi, give us one moment the book is still in the stock room, the books were never unpacked."

I was a little annoyed, but I was going to be on good behavior, but I wasn't sure of her time window. So, I just said

"Ok. I'll be looking at books."

"Thank you." as the book store girl seemed appreciative that I didn't get snippy.

I wasn't sure of my energy around her, it was a tad unsettling, actually I'm usually strict in my ways. I prefer aggressive female in the since of telling me to be aggressive. I never want to offend a female and I never want to ruin a friendship. I prefer a clear signal, a big bright one that they are interested in me or that they want to be pursued by me before any thing on my end becomes aggressive in the since of move making. Not in the since of being aggressive. So, my energy was definitely off, but I watched what isle she was in and I went to the opposite end. I went and said,

"What you looking for?" How to make my favorite meal?" I said that out loud, I also questioned myself why was I saying it out loud.

"No."

"No?"

"Ok."

I thought I really didn't have a comeback for that, so, I just went to explaining,

"They have to get the book from the stock room and it's going to take a second because they have to scan the box in the system."

"Oh, that's fine."

It was at this moment I wondered why I asked her out to eat. Partly I imagine she was cute, partly I guess because the conversation was good. Partly because I was hungry and partly because I didn't want the book store to close.

I really wasn't the one to carry the conversation in a conversation. And, although I just wanted to peel off and go to a different book section, I thought this was my idea, but here as my social anxiety kicked in.

"So, do you know what you might get to eat?"

"No, I've never been there."

"Oh, ok. I always get a burger. I like to see how different people prepare burgers."

"You shouldn't eat a lot of beef."

Her straight forwardness was making me feel awkward but the caring part I liked. I felt slightly conflicted.

"You're right, I definitely need to double up on the roughage and the water. I was internally going in to extreme anxiety over load when the book girl came up says my last name.

"And here you go, sorry it took you so long. I rang it out and processed it for you so if you aren't getting anything else you are good to go."

"Ok, thank you."

I actually needed another book as she grabbed a book as well.

"I needed to get this…" I said "I'll be right there."

I grabbed a book from the business section. We both went to the counter and paid for our books. And exited out of the book store, I grabbed the door for her to walk out. And then we walked towards the restaurant.

I mentioned us not carrying the books and would put them in my car. She waited for me and fixed herself in a mirror. I guess some stuff girls do before they go in to a place. I wasn't sure of her situation or anything, I was still trying to figure out why we were getting something to eat. I asked,

"A patio seat?" she said.

"You sure you don't want to sit in a booth?

"It doesn't matter."

"I thought the weather was nice, why I suggested the patio."

I guess it was like offering a girl who just got her hair done to ride in a convertible. We were shown to a booth. She excused herself and went to the bathroom. I sat there and planted some plants on a game on my phone until she came back. The waiter was putting the water on the table as he backed up and backed in to her.

She said, "Excuse me."

He says, "Oh you can bump me any time. I'll be right back to take your orders."

I was a little uncertain at my response, but I looked at buhl on like this guy type tip. But "we" were out getting something to eat, just two people who enjoyed a summer science program. She was cute, copper complected type, again I felt awkward the energy felt weird.

But on the low I was checking her out. I was wondering. I had let my mind begin to wonder,

as she said "they have burgers."

"Yes ma'am. Bacon cheeseburger, mayo, ketchup, should I get American or

mozzarella? What are you getting?"

She wasn't sure at the time but about time we ordered, she ended up with a shrimp basket with crab cakes or some shii.

My burger was fiyah, we chatted it up for a while and had great conversation. I didn't really particularly care for the dental lecture, but needed it, and appreciated it. We got dessert to go and headed back to the cars. "I enjoyed bumping in to you."

It was weird, felt like we knew each other or I don't know. Perhaps journeyed with one another. I guess just two little black girls who were picked for a science program and knowing what we're now, how ground breaking any thing we do academically is for the generations ahead of us and following our ancestors. I actually love science and wish I wasn't so squeamish. With the lack of black professionals, I feel guilty not being one. We pulled off and about ten minutes later I got a text.

"My book is in your car. Maybe you can bring it tomorrow?"
I was glad she didn't say she needed it now, I guess we both let our days get away from us.

I text back, "no problem."

I was still over all of the place desperately needed a lawyer to do these contracts. I was leaving so much money on the table trying to pick which money to chase. And, I had to cut that shit out. I decided I wanted as many keys as I have hats. The grind was different now, and I just was praying it wasn't too late. I made a little bit of money and then I headed in for the night. Did some creative content before I went to bed and called it a night.

It was about noon when she texted me.

"Hey did you know what time we could meet up so I could get my book?"

"I can drop it off now if you want me to. Just, I need the address."

"Ok, thanks."

She sent the address.

"Ok, I'm like 15 minutes away about a half hour or so."

"Sure, that's fine."

"Great, half an hour."

I was doing some research on customs and I was in line, so although I was fifteen minutes away, I was still fifteen minutes in to what I was doing. I texted her when I was about 5 minutes away. She said.

"The car is in the drive way."

I pulled up about 5 mins later. I pulled in the driveway rolled my window down. And got the book and took it to the door. I rang the bell and she shortly opened it … she had on like this lace leotard thing, with like some biker type shorts, flip flops, very Puerto Rican-ish. Maybe 90-ish, but femal-ish.

"Hey, here's your book."

"Thanks, did you want to come in for a minute?"

I was a bit stunned, because I wasn't really sure why, but,

"Sure." came out of my mouth "let me put my windows up in my car."

I went to my car she stood at the door, I rolled my windows up and locked my door. In my head I was so confused and conflicted but my physical was walking in.

"Thank you for bringing my book."

"No problem."

"You can have a seat. I was just making some tea, did you want some?"

"Some tea? Is it iced tea?"

"Well, if you want it iced, I can add ice."

"I mean, it's a bit toasty out."

I know people heavily in to tea and coffee, so it wasn't that odd. But it being hot was throwing me off a bit.

"Tea? Is it special tea?"

"It's either green or regular."

"I'll take some tea with lemon, I guess." as I chuckled.

"Why is that funny?"

"Um, I don't know, it's just kinda hot out side."

"Oh, I guess."

"Well, I guess your air condition is on like polar bear, so maybe it doesn't really matter." She chuckled.

"So, do you have some where to be?"

"I am always busy." as I responded.

"Oh well, I don't want to hold you up. I don't want your woman to get mad with you."

"My woman?"

"Your man?"

"Um, that I know, I'm single. I can't say I wouldn't like some situations to manifest, but ain't nobody really worried about me being no where's on time or nothing like that."

"Oh, ok."

"And, where your dude?"

"I'm pretty much single."

"Oh, ok. You seem to be a little inviting yet closed off. So, I can understand that."

"What do you mean by that? You had one conversation with me."

"It's the energy, you give, I imagine it's your responsive energy. I guess I will blame it on."

"Oh, ok, that's interesting, I will have to consider that."

My phone alert went off.

"Someone is checking on you?"

Internally I'm perplexed. But, I response and say.

"I actually forgot the game was on and that was the first score alert."

"Oh, did you want to watch the game?"

We walk to the living room and she turns the tv and says "basketball" in to the remote.

I didn't really watch basketball with any one or sports period, just incase some one plays different. I don't want to blame them for the score.

"Did you want some snacks?"

"No, I'm good the tea is ok." I said sarcastically.

She shook her head and asked.

"Was that suppose to be funny?"

I let out a laugh that was heavily breathed through my mouth and nose. Cause her response was just cute and funny.

"Nawhl, I want the tea."

"That's why your team going to lose…"

"Whoa whoa whoa. See now it's time for me to go, I can't have the negative energy over

no tea."

"Whatever."

There were chuckles.

"That's why my team just scored."

"I'm going to make some tacos, to go with the tea, ok?"

I thought that was nice of her. But was heavily confused at why I was at some one's house I just

bumped into yesterday. Although I would have been watching the game.

The food was smelling good and occasionally I would get a glimpse of her walking back

and forth from where I was sitting.

"You drink or smoke? I don't have beer, I have liquor or coolers."

"I don't drink, but 420 is friendly."

I rolled up and was smoking and watching the game. She brought me a plate with the

tacos and some corn and broccoli on the plate. She came back with her plate and sat in the single

chair not next to me on the sofa, I took notice to it but wasn't certain what it meant.

I passed her the el, she took it and puffed it with these little gripped fingers, like she wanted to

taste It or maybe she didn't really smoke I wasn't sure.

The buzzer to the game went off, it was the end of the second quarter and half time.

"So, you like sports, huh?

"Yes, something like that."

"Can I use your rest room?"

"Sure, it's one down the hall, and to your right."

I went to the restroom and when I came back, she was eating ice cream and hadn't really touched her food, she was curled in the chair. Commercials was still on for the half time break. There was a scratch at the door. Do you mind dogs?

"No."

"Can you open that door for me?"

I opened up the door, a little brown dog came from out the opened door and sniffed me. I sat down as the dog hopped up in the chair with her.

"And, we will be right back with the second half."

"I guess I'll stay to the end of the game, if you didn't mind?"

"Well that's what I expected that you were going to watch the game. I didn't think you were going to just watch half."

"Yeah, I guess…"

"Again, thank you for bringing the book."

"No problem."

"You have a lot to do today?"

"I have a lot to do, until I make it to 50k a week."

"I can understand that."

As I remembered to self, "always asked the question back."

"And you, what you up to today?"

"I'm not too sure, take some things off the to do list."

"Oh, ok."

"Do you like the tea?"

"Well after you infused it with the crushed ice. Yes, it was good."

"Now back to the game."

The dog jumped down and knocked her phone off of the table, he trotted back to the room as we both reached for the phone to pick it up.

"Oh, thank you" as I handed it to her.

"Why you sit over there?"

Although, I like women who like to be told what to do, to get to a comfort level of knowing that with a female is a lot of anxiety for me. A lot of women think I'm massively aggressive and I'll be assertive with a woman who wants me to be assertive with her. And, a woman who needs me to be assertive with her, but a woman who wants to contest it, what is my purpose. But again, getting to that point is and can be overwhelming.

"Why don't you sit over here though?"

"Oh, I just always sit here, this is my chair, so I sat in my chair. I'll sit over there."

I smiled big as shii inside and softly on the outside. She cuddled up next to me with her ice cream and under my arm as we watched the game. Which although I am a very animated sports fan, this felt nice.

"Did you play?"

"Yeah, but I didn't know what I know now. I had no idea of team play, I'm just a natural athlete I could have been good at any sport."

"Oh ok."

"Did you play? You seem like you cheered or something."

"What do you think?"

"I don't know."

"Oh, ok."

"You dealt with a female before?"

"Not really my cup of tea."

"Ouch, nothing wrong with an occasional side dish."

"I'm not others."

"What do that mean?"

"It mean, what it mean."

"Well, I don't know what it means."

"Oh, ok."

It was usually here, I lose direction, this moment can go in so many directions when you really want it to go towards one.

"I just think I'm unique in my experience and I don't like really saying I'm an experience."

I gave a complex vulnerable parable response.

I looked away and blew the el. I ran my finger tips on her neck in the back of her ear.

"You have a pretty complexion."

"Thank you."

I rubbed my fingertips down her arm to the top of her hand as I grabbed her hand.

"Air ball, air ball." as the crowd chanted.

She looked at me quizzically, I was just as confused, as I grabbed her chin and kissed her. Went for a signature bottom lip kiss suck move. And rubbed her arm slowly drifting to her hips to her buttock that was exposed by the position she was lying in.

I inhaled the el one more time and putting it in front of her she inhaled and I put it out in the ash tray on the table. I took my sneaks off and put my leg up on the couch. I had on ball shorts on and a promo tee for one of my companies. I took my gun off my hip and put it on the table. She laid on me as we kissed. I was intrigued and wanted to know what type of nipples she had, although she had a lace leotard on she had on a bra that hid them very well. As she laid in between my legs I grabbed her ass and humped her from the bottom. She seem like her sex was about to be good. I slid off one of the shoulders of the leotard when she stopped grinding. To assist me she assisting me taking the one off and helped remove the other. The bra opened in the front and when the last latch was open, in my mouth her breast went. I firmly grabbed the one and engulfed the other. I wanted to see how erect they got, how erect they got by my touch. I ran her nipples on my forehead as we switched positions. I kissed her mouth and then went back to her breast.

I whispered,

"Can I touch her? Does she want me to touch her?"

She faintly said.

"Yes."

I seconded the yes.

"Yes?"

She said.

"Yes." I slid the rest of the leotard off with the tights an I slid my fingers in-between her lips they were moist she was aroused. I placed her nipple back in my mouth and rubbed her soft cup.

"Can I? Can I go in?

I asked.

She took my hand and put me inside of her, then took my face and kissed me. I felt her clench around my fingers.

"Shit."

I bit her lip as I felt her on my fingers.

"You gone keep this tight for me I ask?"

I rubbed her walls. I wanted to see what she responded to, I took the wet juices from her pussy hole and rubbed her clit with them. I was extremely turned on, I squeezed her breast firmly. I switched positions again and took off my shorts.

"Sit here."

I sat her on me and grind-ed the shit out her leaking pussy. She was so wet and you couldn't tell me she wasn't wet for me. She was riding me as I put my thumb on her clit to rub while she rode me. I took my other hand and put her hands on her breast and we squeezed them together. I pinched her nipples. She was bucking, I hoped she was feeling turned on, I hope she was enjoying me. I hoped she was about to cum for me … I turned her back over and got on top of her and slid my fingers inside. I firmly fucked her pussy with my fingers. I tried not to but I knew the hickie would show up with her complexion. I marked her neck while I told her to fuck my fingers…

"Fuck my fingers back, I want you to come all on my fingers….Oh you can't hear me…"
I took my fingers out. And whispered.

"Can I taste her?"
I asked her.

"Game. In an assertive voice.

"Can I taste her?"

"She clean?"

"Yes."

"Your blood clean?"
I know a bitch will tell you anything in this moment, but I rocked with it. I ain't never have no lifetime shit, but can't say I ain't never need an antibody either.

"She clean?"

"Yes." as she reiterated softly, awaiting me to slide down. She was so hard for me … as I put her inside my mouth you hear the gasp. I enjoyed her until she griped the fuck out of my broad shoulders that with women are a plus, with men an insecurity. She let out a "fuck." I climbed back up and hunched her. Mentally I was deep inside of her massaging every layer with every hunch. I hoped for a moan of pleasure, I received some. I hunched until I expelled my sexual energy. I slid my fingers back inside of her. Was she wet for me? I slid back down.

"Has won the game!" The announcer said.
I put her back in my mouth, until I felt her response to me.

"Shit."

She says.

…i rubbed her clit for a few more seconds. Suck popped her titties again and watch her walk naked to her room to get a robe.

When she came back I had put my shorts back on and she was in as I chuckled a silk robe

"Damn, next time, I might have to call you daddy."

I was still confused at this time, she said next time?

I responded with.

"That was good though. That got wet for me?

She smiled.

"I guess I should be going. I hope you enjoy your book. And, thanks for the tea."

"You're welcome. You should text me."

"Oh, I should?"

"Be safe."

"You too."

LOCKED DOWN LOVE

"What are you watching?"

I'd just waken up, I was a tad restless the night before, so I missed first rec.

"I don't know, the television is just on really."

"Oh ok, where's cousin?"

"Yours or mines, well they are both down medical."

"Oh ok. I wish football was on but at the same time I don't."

"Come in, you can watch until rec was over."

She scooted to the side of the bunk.

"Ain't no crabby patties in here." We both chuckled.

I really wasn't thinking anything sexual, more of a height thing.

"Here, let me put my legs in back of you."

She was a tad shorter. I randomly said, was and how I missed the wasp that were building outside of my window in the other pod. As I thought of Tutor Pods my educational learning app and site.

"I'll be back I'm going to take a shower. You can watch what you like."

She and her cousin had been so kind to me, little angels if you will. I was watching my routine programming had I'd been home. She came back and I got up to leave the room.

"Girl you don't have to leave. We all seen and have the same thing."

She had already friend zoned me, so I wasn't thinking of her in that manner. But she began to dry off and lotion up.

"Nice thighs."

"You think so?"

"Yeah."

I rubbed her leg and she giggled.

"That tickles."

"Oh, I'm sorry."

I touched her thigh again, but this time I went closer, upwards.

"Stop playing."

I'd forgot she said she had girlfriends, so I don't think she was completely new to this.

"Want me to kiss it?"

"You can."

She blocked the view of the window with a towel, unless you looked hard, I couldn't really be seen. I put my mouth on her and she taste nice and clean, she moaned and said,

"Dammit."

Her clit, I slid my fingers inside of her. She was tight for me. I seen her leg start to get weak so I slid my fingers out and finished up with my tongue until she climaxed. She actually leaked on the floor, not too much, but enough to stoke my ego. She finished putting her clothes back on and we never really mentioned our moment.

UPPER CLASS LOVE

I was headed Ninety-Five South. I'd decided to check in to the hotel since I would be down here for a few days. But, I couldn't find it, my gps read that I was five minutes away, but I damn sure didn't see it. I circled around quit a few times. I decided to get something to eat so headed to a convenience store. I almost bumped into this BMW pulling in to the gas station. I was pulling into the parking lot, I'd gotten hungry and frustrated. I found a spot and parked and headed in the store. I was tapping the screen for my meatball sub. When I heard,

"You were going to hit my shit, huh green?"

I'd forgot that was a term but heard it a few times since I'd been home. I turned around and smiled.

"Nah, my skills is better than that. And ma, I can't afford a seven series just yet."

"But the Porsche is nice." She says.

"Base model, base model, hug?"

She opened her arms, she stay hugging someone like they're little.

"Good to see you."

"You too." She replied.

"Yeah, glad that's over."

"That part."

She got her soup and I ordered a soup.

"What are you up to?"

"Well headed to Maryland for the weekend, but at the moment looking for this hotel that

I   apparently can't find."

"What's the name of it?"

I showed her the phone and the reservation.

"Oh, I'm headed that way, follow me and you can just turn off in five miles or so, it's in a roundabout, probably why you didn't see it."

"Oh, thanks, just waiting for my food."

"So, what have you been up to?"

"You know me, business, business, business, and yourself? Have you found something that interested you?"

"Yeah, a few things mainly realty."

They called my number for my food. I got my food and headed to the car.

"If you want to hang out with me tonight you can."

"Maryland, huh?"

"Yeah, all girls club. But, I'll keep you close and safe, if you want to go."

"Sure, I'll go."

"Okay, I'll probably head out like ten thirty or so, you can meet me here or if you're easy to find or, if you want to meet me there, I'll put you on my vip list. Either here or there."

"Put me on the list, so just in case, I wouldn't want to hold you up."

"Solid, here put your number in my phone."

She made my phone ring and headed to her car. I got into my car and drove up to her car. I pulled up next to her so she could lead me to the hotel. It was about a four-mile drive, she turned into the hotel it, was in the cut, a cul-de-sac. I don't know if I would have found it had she not shown it to me. Definitely in the ducky.

We pulled up so our driver sides could be next to one another. We put down our windows down.

"Thank you."

"You're welcome. See you later."

"Yes, okay, until then."

She pulled off in her dark green 7 series BMW.

I checked in after parking the car. I went up to my room. I showered and laid down for a bit. I awakened to a text.

I'll meet you there. I'll call you when I'm in the parking lot."

"Sure." I texted back.

I was thankful that she let me know what moves or how we were moving. I continued to rest up for a little while longer. I finally got up and pulled out my lay for the night. I still didn't get dressed until I was a block away. So, I put what I was wearing in one of the store bags and showered up again. I'd slept a bit hard. After showering, I lotion-ed up and threw on my driving clothes. I headed to the car, I left her name and for her to get a key if she came to the hotel just in case. I headed to the club house and got there about fifteen to twenty minutes. I got a text when I got to the parking lot.

"Be there in a half an hour."

"Oh, okay. Let me know, I'll meet you."

I was chilling for the most part, I hadn't been out in a while. It felt good to be out and I loved being in this environment. It was beautiful to be amongst black women, black women that were productive. In my city I haven't really found such circle. I always think it's because I'm kind of a southerner, until I'm around the deep southerners with the true southern accents. I headed out front to the door about twenty minutes later and waited for her in the car. She pulled up as I was pulling on my blunt. She shook her head and smiled. She very rarely showed emotions, I some times thought she showed me how difficult I am to read emotionally. She got out of the car. She looked cute, capris, sneaks and a polo popped collar. I smiled, she had a clutch, a sporty type clutch. She definitely was my type of cute. I walked with her and she got her arm band for the night. I made sure she was okay drink wise and we tried to talk loud or whisper in one another's ear.

"Thank you, for inviting me."

"Thank you, for showing me where the hotel was located."

"No problem."

She snugged up to me for a while and then I excused myself.

I asked.

"Are you going to be okay for a while?"

She said.

"Yes, and asked why?

I told her.

"You'll see in a while and don't let anyone really sit in our reserve area. Just say it's reserved.

She said, "okay."

I grabbed her hand and kissed her cheek and went to change my clothes. About fifteen minutes went passed and the host announced my performance name. This was about my third performance. I performed for my fifteen mins. I thought I did half decent but I'd still wish I'd done it in my younger days, but I was making the best of it. This last run.

"I heard, five, four, three, two, and... one."

I walked off the floor and went to changed back into my clothes. I shortly walked back to my table. She was smiling and shaking her head. I chuckled and flopped down and snugged closely like we were sitting before I left. She leaned into me from an angle and we watched the rest of the performances. I excused myself, I was still doing my signature departure. So, I had to say my see you laters. We had shows all weekend. I said see you to the those I say it to.

I asked her, "are you ready to leave?"

She said, "sure."

She scooted sideways out the booth and I walked behind her, holding her waist until we got to the door. I opened the door and we headed to the parking lot.

It was about five of two am.

"Are you alright to drive? I know you didn't have too much to drink or you can come to the hotel or text me when you get home."

"I think its best if I come to the hotel because I am a half hour away."

"Sure, I guess, I'll follow you, you know the area better. The hotel was like eight minutes away. She knew the area better and took a back road that lead to the side of the hotel. We parked side by side I waited for her and I grabbed the shrimp and chicken platters that I'd got. I got my blunt out the car.

"You're greedy." she says.

"Not really. But, I'm about to be with this food."

I put my dutch in my ear and then she took it and put it in my shirt pocket as we were walking through the door. The concierge greeted us and said "good night."

I said, "dang. We could've valeted."

"No. That's ok, I really don't like others to drive or park my cars.

"Oh plural, huh?"

"Of course."

We got up to the suite and I tapped the key card and opened the door. I put my food in the microwave told her to get comfortable. Although I wanted to dance waddling on the floor was quite disgusting, so I definitely was headed to the shower. I showered for about ten minutes she was on the couch watching tv while I showered and I put on some shorts and a tee. I grabbed my food, I offered her some, she took a chicken wing and a napkin. We talked for a while it was close to four.

I told her, "you can have the bed. I'll stay in the living room."

"She said, there's no need for that I don't feel unsafe with you."
That always made me feel like I was a good person when people say they feel safe with me or fall asleep around me.

We shut the tv off. I had extra shorts and a tee. She opted for the tee, she had on like boy shirts, but her ass was very fat, so her cheeks didn't give them panties no chance I was definitely tired. Although I'd gotten tight body, my stamina was not just there yet. While those thoughts were creeping in my head.

She said, "You did well.
I chuckled and said.

"Thanks."

Because I had a lot to do, but I didn't know if it was too late in the game to give a great performance. I turned down my side of the bed, she turned down her side and I guess I was way more exhausted then I knew, because I'm pretty certain that I was probably snoring five minutes later.

About four hours after that, I softly woke up and all of those cheeks pressed against me, so I pulled back and cozied and they found me again I disconnected again. But she snuggled against me again. Still I drifted off again and wrapped my arms around her, she put the top of her torso against my chest her warmth felt nice I really wasn't thinking about this, heck, I didn't even expect to run in to her. I really didn't know if she wanted me to make a move or forgot where she was, she turned to me and said,

"Good morning."

In the middle of saying that I remember that I didn't say morning any more, so immediately after,

I said. "Top of the top."

She kissed me unexpectedly,

"You know, I'm married right?"

"Yes, I know."

"So, this could never be anything serious."

I had a flashback and said.

"An experience."

"Yes, I would like to experience you, is that okay?"

"Not really, I kind of don't like being an experience."

She touched my face, I kissed her bottom lip, to a sucking her lip and caressed her body, her lips were nice. She corresponded sucking my top lip, I placed my hand on her body and inside her vagina lips, her clitoris had swelled to welcome me. It got me excited that she'd been excited by my touch, she sucked my bottom lip more hungrily. I positioned her as I turned to my back her on top of me in a mounted position I grind-ed into her, mentally I was deep inside her rotating my hips. I began like an amusement park ride that's just beginning, grinding firmly, she began leaking on me. I put her breast in my mouth, she must've have compassion that I was shorter than she, she met me coming down. I loved the way her nipples hardened in my mouth. As she responded grinding hard in to me. Mentally, I was deep and she felt me inside every inch of her, she had me by a couple inches, but I still needed to display my strength, I placed my arm around the back of her torso and flipped her to her back and positioned myself on top of her strongly I got really turned on as I remembered how she sits femininely while sitting beside me. I grind-ed deeply and hard. I almost got lost giving her pleasure, wrapped up in mine. I slowed down and slid down and put her in my mouth in position. She instantly grabbed my head and enjoyed me

She grind-ed her clit into my mouth, she moaned and let out some expletives.

"Damn you feel so good. I'm about to cum." I hummed with my mouth full, she exploded in my mouth. I felt like a master masseuse, her body went to full relax.

"Cum for me." she said.

I put her hands between my legs and she tandem-ly helped me to my climax. We laid there for about twenty minutes and then got our days started.

A CHESTER GIRL

It was about seven months after discharge. I'd just gotten an eight hundred cc Kawasaki motorcycle bike and the rights to carry my fire arm back. I'd decided to go to the other city, I just open up one of my studios. I know I wasn't going to feel like getting gas in the morning. I pulled into the gas station, put my helmet on the top of my head and then placed it on the bike. I selected the gas year and removed the nozzle and decided I wanted something to drink after all. I walked up to the store and grabbed a soda and headed back to the bike. An all tinted out Bronco pulls up and slightly alarmed me by pulling in so close, but didn't hit me. I heard my name called with a smile behind it. I turned around and chuckled.

"Hey, hi, how are you?"

Things picked up for me tremendously after discharge and the charges were thrown out, dropped, dismissed and expunged, I didn't mind linking with the crew. We all kept in touch, but not really through any devices.

"How have you been?"

I actually never forgot her and wear the string ring around my finger.

She said, "I'm good."

I heard the click to the pump on my bike. I excused myself and walked back to the pump and removed the nozzle and grabbed a card out of my back pack. I straddled my bike and walked it next to her Bronco as she finished up in the store. She was still cute, innocent type look. I can't really truly vouch for innocent, but she looks it. She was pretty.

"What are you doing over here?" She asked.

"You know, I'm a little everywhere. But nah, I grabbed a spot near the college."

"Oh, ok. that's what's up. I opened the tea, began drinking the tea, she realized I still had the string on my finger.

"You still wear that?"

I tee heed and smiled.

"Yeah something like that."

"Oh, ok, what you about to get into?"

"Not much, some editing and shit like that."

"Oh ok, well, it was good seeing you."

I asked.

"Can I get my hug?" she turned my torso, I actually decided to get off the bike to open the car door for her.

She said. "Thank you. And said you were always sweet."

"And, you were always cute, ever since the med room honestly. Honesty is very attractive especially hard honesty. I'm a very word is bond type so it just stood out and she's just quite easy on the eyes. She put the seat belt on and I gave her a card and the personal number I wrote on the back. I let her know the days that I'm usually down this way.

"Oh, you have cards?"

"I've always got cards."

She looked slightly impressed, but I did always have cards. I kissed her cheek.

I told her. "Be good and safe."

She said. "I will."

I walked my bike backwards and had I started riding earlier in life I probably would have showed off and did a wheelie. But instead, I did the biker turn signal, signaled and rode off with one hand on my leg and kind of on one side of the bike. I rode off as impressive as I could. Not that she was watching.

The plan of the studios was coming along, I'd open four of them and couldn't wait to see a global map and the international lay out. I had some ads I needed to work on and probably worked on them for the next six hours when I noticed I was starving and missed two texts, one was from my lil young buhl and the other her asking what I was up to, I was sorry that I had missed the calls. It was a tad after eight when I decided to text her back.

Eight o'clock is still a tricky time when you don't know someone's situation. I text her back.

At the moment, probably about to order some dinner and get back to what I do. I was searching the delivery apps for about fifteen minutes, when she replied.

"I made stuffed shells, would you for me to bring you some or you can come by and get some."

I really didn't expect a response, but I didn't expect a text originally either.

"Um sure, you can drop some off."

"Okay give me about a half an hour. You are near the college, right?"

"Yes, I'll text you the address. I was thrown off by even bumping into her and wouldn't let my thoughts run away with where they wanted to go. I text her the address and then got back to some editing. I'd finally got into the rhythm of creating ads and had a good seasonal rotation.

I was about forty minutes in drafting this ad when she rang my phone. I got to the phone on the third ring, she repeated the address. I laughed and headed to the door. She was still in her car when I reached down stairs. I opened the door and waved to her.

"This is the address."

I told her she could come in for a while, so, she parked behind the bike after I pointed to the spot. She looked cute, she had a Fendi bag with some Fendi pants type style, with an extra fitting blouse on. She opened the back door to get the container of food. I walked over to grab the containers and closed the car door. I headed to the door to the building and punched in the code, opened the door and entered the building. My buildings usually have a dormitory area, work out area which can double as a dance studio, a photography video area and an editing bay and a audio recording area. We walked through the dormitory living space.

"Oh, this is nice." She commented.

"Thank you."

We headed to the kitchen area. I advised her she could have a seat and let her know she could have a drink. I usually kept the bar well stocked, mainly because I didn't drink. I wasn't sure if she was much of a drinker but she knows it was available. I went to the cabinets to get a plate, had she not been there, I would have definitely used styrofoam plates, it looked seasoned pretty well as I was transferring the food from the container to the plate. I was still anticipating to see if it was tasteful or not.

"Are you eating any?"

"I'll just have some of yours." She replied.

I grabbed another plate, I guess I should have asked should I have put this on the stove, or in oven or was it going in the microwave. I covered the plates and put them in the microwave and continued to ask her how she had been.

She said. "Everything is ok, not great, but not bad."

"Well I guess that's good."

She said. "As long as I have God, there's not much to complain about."

I understood that perspective and mind set. The microwave alerted that the food was at a warm temperature or that it was finished heating up.

I asked. "Do you want any juice, soda or water?"

She said. "I'll have whatever you're drinking."

I grabbed two juices and glasses and we headed to the couch in front of the television and discussed a few topics. I showed her the rest of the studio. She shared some of her dreams with me, conversation was nice.

She asked. "Can I use the restroom?"

I straightened up the plates we used.

She asked. "What are you about to get into?"

I told her. "I have a taste for some pie so probably headed to the store."

"Some pie huh?"

"Yes, sweet potato or apple."

"Oh, I thought that was code for something else."

"Nah, no code. I can catch 'em, but I ain't never been able to keep them. Look I couldn't keep you."

She walked close to me and asked for a hug. I hugged her she felt nice and warm as always. I don't know why but I went in for the kiss and she returned it. Shit was like falling into heaven, it was so soft and warm. I pulled her tighter. I wasn't too sure where this was going to lead, but I was definitely letting it flow.

"You think the pie can wait?" She asked.

"I remember you saying that…"

I cut her off. "Wanted some of you, yeah I definitely did."

"Do you still want some?"

"You're in my arms aren't you. Why? Can I have some?"

For me it's about permission. I don't know, but once a woman gives me permission to park my manners, I don't know, just something about a woman giving you permission to explore their body.

I backed her over to the couch and we went from vertical to horizontal. I laid on her and immediately tried to line up our warmest parts. I continued kissing her as I unbuttoned her blouse, it was tan and like a silk texture, almost sheer see though. I reached in the back for her bra clasps.

She said. "They're in the front."

There were three clasps, I unhooked them and began rubbing my lips on her nipples. I felt them respond to me and my ego enjoyed every bit of the response I didn't know which one I wanted more, the left or the right. I was like a dj on the turntables, sucking each one, feeling them get firmer in my mouth, hearing her respond. That shit turned me on with each moan, my shit was on throb city and it was all her fault. I moved down to her stomach and naval. I subtly bit under her belly button as I slid my hands down the inside of her pants to begin rubbing them, I buried my head in her triangle and I asked her for clear certainty.

"You sure."

She said. "Yes." I bit the inside her thighs and buried my head in between her legs like I was using her thighs for ear muffs or headphones. I sucked on her pussy lips like it was a popsicle. She exhaled a relief of passion I wanted to do a good job and I think I was doing ok she grabbed my locs and bucked back hard, slow grinding back. That shit was sending me bonkers. I always kinda envied men being able to feel a woman and this was that moment that feeling kicks in

7-9

"See you tomorrow."

"Yes, see you tomorrow."

I hung up the phone. I was still shoe stringing things together but they were starting to connect way better. I was seeing revenue from the sites. So, I think momentum was on its way. I finished packing, I had a flight in the morning. I really didn't want to go, but I was going. I'd never been to the A, so that was also a plus. But these trade shows, at first, I didn't get their purpose, nor mine, but now I see their importance.

The crowd funding group I was a part of wanted me to go. I just felt like they weren't concentrating on the end user as much as they should, among some other aspects and things. I totally get that they want everyone to be self-sufficient independently but you still need a business infrastructure. I still needed to write some things for my master's application. But the most important thing was making money through these sites. I just needed orders and more orders. I finished packing. I still hadn't found my style, nor had I had any money to go shopping, so I had to keep piecing things together until things started really rolling in, which I really hoped God had planned soon. I put my bags next to the door, so I could head to the airport early in the morning. Rolled a L and just thought about where I was in life. Life really throws curve balls at you. And, I don't know if I am partly insane but I am glad I had the lord and goals to continue to go forward.

I smoked the el and said my prayers and headed to sleep. I slept pretty decent, and thought I got a good amount of rest. Next thing you know the alarm was going off at three twenty, I laid in the bed for bout ten minutes. After that I pushed myself through an experience that I'd been begging for.

I freshened up, put on some comfy wear for the plane, grabbed my bag and headed to the train. I got on the train headed to the airport, took about ten minutes. I knew I was going to be a little early so I got off the stop early and watched some videos and smoked the rest of my bud before I got to the airport. Things were so crazy, not necessarily in a bad way, probably more in a chaotic disorder way. I wasn't going to fret over it much, just was going to focus and just continue to stay consistent and not too hard on myself. The bus headed to the airport was coming in a while, I gathered my stuff and was ready. The bus came around the bin, I flicked my stinger to the ground and wiped it out … threw the strap of the gym bag across my shoulder. And waited for the bus to slow down. I got on, it was someone I was familiar with so I didn't have to pay fare.

"Hey. Where you headed?"

"Oh, to this trade show for these bags."

"Oh, ok."

"How you been?"

"I've been good and yourself?

"I can't complain."

"Oh, ok."

She walked close to me and asked for a hug. I hugged her she felt nice and warm as always. I don't know why but I went in for the kiss and she returned it. Shit was like falling into heaven, it was so soft and warm. I pulled her tighter. I wasn't too sure where this was going to lead, but I was definitely letting it flow.

"You think the pie can wait?" She asked.

"I remember you saying that…"

I cut her off. "Wanted some of you, yeah I definitely did."

"Do you still want some?"

"You're in my arms aren't you. Why? Can I have some?"

For me it's about permission. I don't know, but once a woman gives me permission to park my manners, I don't know, just something about a woman giving you permission to explore their body.

I backed her over to the couch and we went from vertical to horizontal. I laid on her and immediately tried to line up our warmest parts. I continued kissing her as I unbuttoned her blouse, it was tan and like a silk texture, almost sheer see though. I reached in the back for her bra clasps.

She said. "They're in the front."

There were three clasps, I unhooked them and began rubbing my lips on her nipples. I felt them respond to me and my ego enjoyed every bit of the response I didn't know which one I wanted more, the left or the right. I was like a dj on the turntables, sucking each one, feeling them get firmer in my mouth, hearing her respond. That shit turned me on with each moan, my shit was on throb city and it was all her fault. I moved down to her stomach and naval. I subtly bit under her belly button as I slid my hands down the inside of her pants to begin rubbing them, I buried my head in her triangle and I asked her for clear certainty.

"You sure."

She said. "Yes." I bit the inside her thighs and buried my head in between her legs like I was using her thighs for ear muffs or headphones. I sucked on her pussy lips like it was a popsicle. She exhaled a relief of passion I wanted to do a good job and I think I was doing ok she grabbed my locs and bucked back hard, slow grinding back. That shit was sending me bonkers. I always kinda envied men being able to feel a woman and this was that moment that feeling kicks in

"Well, I'mma go back here and sit down. It's mad early and I didn't have any coffee."

I really don't drink coffee, but I was mad faded and didn't feel like really chatting it up with any one.

"Aiyte, well talk to you later."

"You too, have a good day though."

"Ok, ok."

I went and sat down. It was a short ride. I was there in like five minutes. I got to the airport and headed to the terminal that I needed to depart from. I had about 45 minutes or so before they were calling for boarding. I decided to go over the goods and products and the numbers that I feel like we should really be looking at for the consumers. I wasn't going to press the issue, I had to press forward the way I knew how and what was best for me.

About ten minutes in to looking at my, I felt a soft tap on my shoulder. I moved my headphones from my ear and looked up and got a cheese smile.

"Heyyy, Aren't you.."

There was a hesitant drawn out.

"Tomboi tech?"

"Tomboy tech.. yeah 7 to 9."

" … yeah.."

I giggled. "Hi."

"Hello… how are you?"

"Um, I'm good and yourself?"

I was totally caught off guard. And, had no idea what to do or say. I guess this will be a responsive conversation. I thought to myself.

"I'm good."

"Where you headed?"

"Oh me, um to a as the name had escaped me, um a trade show."

"Oh, ok."

"Flight 519?"

"Yeah, flight 519."

"Oh, ok."

"Ok what are you doing?"

"Editing some content. And I am not the best at grammar."

She moved her bag and her purse to where I was sitting.

"I'll take a look at it for you."

"So what problem are you having?"

"Well, I imagine, I have a problem with phrasing the call of action and being grammatically correct."

She said. "Oh."

Softly drew a line through what I'd written and corrected it.

"That should be a strong enough call to action."

I looked at it what she'd written and agreed.

"Wow, thanks."

"You're welcome, no problem. So, how long are you down there for."

"Just the weekend."

"And, yourself?

"Yes, just the weekend, had switched some days with someone, so had the weekend off."

"Well hope that's a good thing."

"Well wanted to go later, so I could escape the cold weather, a little later?"

But, going home is always nice."

"Yes that's right, no doubt."

"I sat quiet."

"So, a trade show?

"Yeah. African crowd funding. And going to look at some leather goods. Preferably back backs and bags. Those are the things that I know how to sell, I am not really familiar with African culture and who buys it and the way I am suggesting to market it. Perhaps I don't know how to convey what I am trying to say. Or they just aren't listening. And that's fine."

"Oh well good luck."

"Thank you."

They called for us to board the plane, I was in business class, she was in first class.

"Well enjoy your weekend."

"You too."

"Hey, take my number, just in case you need anything."

"Ok, sure."

She read her number aloud, as I type it in to my key pad. And hit send. Her phone rang.

"Got it."

"Ok, cool."

"Ok, I smiled."

And asked. Are you okay with your bags?"

"Yes."

"You sure?"

I asked in a I don't mind, being polite, I am a strong tomboy manner.

She said. "I've got it.

In an independent type of way. I couldn't get too unfocused, so I headed to my seat. I was still faded as shii, I just fell asleep quite instantly. About thirty minutes left in the flight, I woke up.

The trade show wasn't until Sunday and it was Friday. I had a lot of time to think. Figured I'd take the camera out and definitely had to hit the hood.

Thirty minutes passed and we were instructed to remain in our seats, we were landing soon. I was anxious about the way things with business was going, but they say being anxious is living in the future. I needed to slow down and deal with the present. There were so many things I just I imagine I wasn't doing like keeping a legit calendar. We are now landing. The pilot said the city, weather and time. I had to get my bearings, I'd never been to this city and needed to stay focused. We landed and departed the plane. I only had one bag to wait for, I headed to baggage claim. Grabbed my bag. Headed to the car, pointed my finger in the air, to the driver who had my name on the placard. We headed to the car. I seen her get in the car that was waiting for her.

Looked like a friend or a family member, she smiled like how you see your family who loves

you, who is happy to see you, to see you are safe. One that was going to have fun for the

weekend. She seen me get in to car and smiled and wave. I wondered how someone could be so

happy. Slightly smiled and waved back, her innocence that was protected by being love was

relevant and blatant.

The car was headed to the hotel. It took about twelve minutes. Arrived at the hotel and

grabbed everything, grabbed my bag. Walked through the vestibule, checked in to the hotel. I

booked a session with a trainer that I was very interested in being stretched out by. I had that

session in about two hours. I had to go on the hunt for the bud. Hit my phone. Who around?

Niguhs, hit back. I ain't really know too many people, and I ain't have too much shii on me. So,

I put my location on for a delivery … grabbed my delivery, rolled up and blew…

I headed to the trainer, got to the trainer's location and had a beautiful session. Put my

shoulder back in place and flexed my hip and stretched my hip out real nice. Having hyper

flexibility is neat some times and sucks at others. Session was awesome. Went and grabbed

something to eat and headed it back to the hotel. For the next couple of hours, I edited and then

worked on sites all night. Was a bit restless but was trying to get as much designing and

developing done as possible. I stayed up until about three am designing sites, adding an inner

league amongst the business. Adding the inner league was the task at hand. I needed to design

an easy registry for teams and players. At a central location. I eventually was tired enough to

fall asleep, woke up to my phone going off, 7-9. I looked at the phone

"I answered. Hey.

"Hey...were you busy?"

"No, not really."

"Well, did you want to do lunch."

"Sure."

"Ok, how's one thirty?"

"Sure, one thirty, is fine."

It was eleven twelve.

"Where are you."

"Where am I?"

I know I'd been sleep, but I had to remember, that I wasn't in a city that I was familiar with and just because she seemed sweet and wholesome, doesn't mean that she was sweet and wholesome.

"Yo, you ain't no robber is you?"

She chuckled. "A robber? No, I'm not no robber."

"Oh, ok."

I told her the name of the hotel that I was staying.

"I'll be there to get you."

Stranger danger was alerting me. I definitely came back with the.

"I can meet you."

"No, it's no problem. I'll come get you. Did you want anything in particular?"

"Nah, not really it's your city you can choose."

"Ok, 1:30."

"Yeah, 1:30."

My head hit the pillow. I really needed to be a little more social, but I truly didn't mind not being social. Plus, I had no social shit to wear. I drifted off for another hour or so. 12:50 the clock read when I re opened my eyes. Peeled myself out of the bed. Started the shower. Took a extreme steamy hot shower. Threw some shorts on and a company hoodie. It was 1:22 when she texted. Almost there. She seemed quite chipper. I loved her energy, I did, but people like her made me feel old. I text back, I'm ready. I hadn't been able to get the colognes, so I was still messing with the oils. Oiled down in my signature oil, blue Abercrombie. Put my hair in a ponytail. I rolled up and blew an el 'til she got here. Text came through, about ten minutes in to my el.

"Downstairs."

I walked through the door. She beeped, she was in a luxury SUV.

"Hi."

"Hello."

"Do you ever cheer up?"

"Just a lot on my mind."

"Oh, ok, I can understand that."

"Food."

"Food."

I repeated back.

"Yes, lunch."

"Food should make you happy."

"Oh, ok. Yes... nah I'm good. This is just mad weird, you don't think?"

"Yeah, I do, but I don't know, I texted you if you wanna go for something to eat."

"No doubt."

She pulled off, looked over the steering wheel the way females do.

"You drink?"

"Nah, bud only …"

"Oh, you one of them?"

"I guess. Never liked the taste of alcohol."

"Ok, no, no judging."

"Oh, ok. That's good. So, what's on your mind?"

"I guess the trade show, business all that stuff. Nothing that I can truly control. I guess I try to calculate a lot of things you know, so just trying to calculate and I guess exponent fast.

"Exponent. That's funny. Double up?"

"Double up."

She pulled in to the restaurant parking lot.

"I hope that you like the food."

"No doubt."

They had a bunch of stuff on the menu, chicken, fish, meatloaf, bar-b-cued items. I just got some mac and cheese, some greens and some mashed potatoes. She got some seaweed wrap type of contraption and a veggie slushy. I picked up her slushy and looked at it, I said.

"I guess."

"What? It's good."

"Yeah no doubt, it looks ok. I just haven't got to the healthy side just yet."

"Oh, ok."

We sat and talked about business, life and love. For about a hour and half. Conversation was nice. Intellectual. I'd never been in such realms on a conversation on that level.

The check came. I pulled my wallet out paid the bill. This was not in the weekend balance, I was internally cringing at the balance.

"Oh, thank you." She kissed my cheek.

I am going to use the rest room, I'll be right back."

"Ok, I'll be at the car."

"No, wait for me."

"Oh, ok."

I sat back down in the booth. I chuckled. I just wanted to blow. Shi I like to blow bud in any city. I intake the city and shii I don't know. My phone rang, so, I walked to the door. I waited at the door. She came out of the restroom.

"You just couldn't wait."

I pointed to the phone.

"Nah, my phone rang. As I put it on speaker."

"Yo playa, you made it, you gotta come through tonight or what my niguh ….?"

"Yo shit not even in the budget, my niguh."

"Here you go, you the one wanted your own business, wanted to leave the 9 to 5. I remember you putting knots in your hat 80 cell phones. While getting checked down.

"Well shit, niguh, that ain't the current case." It ain't gone kill you, I promise it'll come back to you niguh. Aiyte, I'll figure how to get there."

"Aiyte niguh, see you in a few hours niguh…"

"I can't get no sleep …"

"Niguh, you and them naps."

"Yo, it's 9 am some wheres."

"You right, no doubt."

I disconnect the phone call.

"Oh, you know people?"

"Nah, not really, not really like that, you know the computer make the world small."

"Oh, ok."

I felt like I should do an invite.

"Did you want to go?"

"If you would like for me to go."

"To be honest. I'm just thinking about this trade show. Everything else just seem mad

extra. I want to pick the right exact products items would sell out immediately."

"Don't think about it so hard."

"Easier said than done."

"Ok, I won't press you."

I kinda knew that I was going out but I really didn't know I was going to be going out with

someone. My wardrobe was the thinnest. Especially to be going out with someone.

After a short type of drive, we pulled up to the hotel.

"So what time should I pick you up?"

"Ten thirty is fine. I really can't stay out too long. I need to prepare for tomorrow. The

trade show is at 1:00."

"Ok."

"Ok.

I hopped out the car.

"Aiyte."

"Aiyte. 10:30."

"10:30."

It was 4:30.

"Hey, you do know what type of club it is?"

"Yes, I know. I could kinda tell from your conversation at The Kitchen."

"Oh, ok."

She smiled, her smile was pretty.

"I was just asking, I didn't know."

"Ok, see you later."

"See you later."

She looked over the steering wheel and pulled out the hotel drive way.

I had some registering to do for the trade show. I headed to my room and got to doing some of the registering and looking at some of the products and the designers. I decided to watch some tv and grab a nap. I woke up at 9:45. I missed the text.

"Hey, are we still on for tonight?"

It had come through at 9:15.

I text back. "Yes, getting dressed now."

A few minutes went passed and a smiley face and an ok came through.

"See you soon."

"Ok."

"Ok."

She didn't seem like the type to smoke, so I just smoked until she got there. Then I figure I'll blow in the parking lot. It was 10:35, a text came through.

"Downstairs."

"Ok, here I come."

I came downstairs to the car. She was in a luxury sedan. I shook my head and just tried not to smile but thought that it was some real g shii. Had my usual prep type shii on. I couldn't really see her outfit when I got in the car. She kissed my cheek when I got in the car. I really didn't understand how to take that kiss on the cheek. I just responded with a.

"Hey."

"You look cute and smell nice." She said.

I chuckled. "Thank you. You smell nice."

It was a peach type scent. Made me want some cobbler.

"So, where is the place at?"

"Oh. Yeah, hold up."

She began to drive out the parking space slowly. I gave her the address, she put it in to the nav system. Twenty-seven minutes was the estimated times that it showed with a few possible routes.

"Oh wow, I guess we should have left earlier."

"I don't mind. I am just not really a night person."

"Oh ok."

It was quiet, pretty much the rest of the drive there. I started a conversation with.

"Do you date females?"

"Look where I am from. She responded.

"That doesn't mean anything."

"Nah, not really. I don't, I don't know. You're cute though."

"Oh, I'm cute. Yeah, you're cute."

"I'm cute, huh?

"You're cute too. You have a beautiful smile. I'm a sucker for a nice smile."

"Oh, thank you."

She smiled and blushed, then she asked.

"Do you date females?

"Yes, something like that."

"Something like that?"

"Nah, I date them. I just rarely am compatible with someone."

"Oh, ok."

We talked about relationships for the rest of the ride.

"Destination in 4 minutes." The nav system alerted us.

I finished getting dressed. Earrings, watch, type stuff. Pulled the fitted out the bag. She pulled

in the parking lot and found a spot. She grabbed her shoes from the back seat and put them on, I

walked to her side of the car and waited for her. She looked cute. She had shoes on with a

blouse. With a purse to match the shoes. I hit my homie. Yo, I'm at the door. I paid for us to get in the club, my homie got to the door as I paid... I gave my homie the this is in my pockets look.

"Stop bitchin' niguh, you finally made it down here."

"Yeah niguh, down this mf huh... no doubt. Let's go..."

"Let's go ... you finnuh bless us...?

"You know if the mood hit me."

My homie had a table for me and directed me to the table ...

"My niguh..."

"My niguh, thanks..."

The homie shook my hand, put a dub a bud in my hand...

"My niguh ..."

"See, I told you that shit gone back to you ..."

"Stop fucking wit them lame asses..."

"Niguh ..."

"Niguh, I know, glad to see you down here..."

"No doubt..."

"No doubt..."

"How you got a date already, niguh ..."

She put her finger in my belt loop ...I was about to introduce her but she cut me off and said.

"Hi."

"Hi."

"Well yawl table right there..."

"No doubt."

We sat at the table…

"I see you tomboy popular…"

"Nah…I know a few real ones though."

We sat and talked and took in the scene. The dj started going off, I excused my self and headed to the floor. My homie pointed to me, I pointed to my homie and started dancing… I danced for a good 40 minutes and came back to the table. She was ordering a glass of wine.

"And, here I thought you had no energy."

"Nah, I always have energy to dance I guess."

"Ok …"

"You ready?"

"If you're ready."

"Ok, no doubt."

"I'll be right back. Let me peace out to my peoples and I'll be right back."

"Ok, take your time."

She held up the wine. I came about 15 minutes later. She took my hand and intertwined her fingers in mine. We walked to the car. I opened the door for her. We got in headed to the hotel arrived about 30 minutes later.

"You ok to drive home?"

"Are you flirting with me?"

"No, just checking on your safety."

"No, you right though, I am a bit tired. Let me park ok…"

She parked the car.

… to be continued.

Parking Spot

I'd circled around the block around six times already and couldn't find a spot with in four square miles. I think that's the measurement, well two square miles, two up, two over and squared by two. I promise, I was driving for like 20 minutes looking for a spot and finally. I didn't really want to hold up traffic but finally a space opened up. I sat as the driver pulling out dang near was doing the three-point turn to get out of the spot. My vehicle was a tad smaller so it shouldn't take me as long to park, although I was a bit conscious of holding up traffic for the car to pull out and for me to park. I was hoping that it wouldn't take me too long. The car finally got all the way out of the spot. Now, I was attempting to park in the spot. Took me a few minutes, not too long. I parked and then I sat in the car for a second. I really didn't want to use my card to pay for a parking ticket, so I looked around to see if I see a parking meter maid, I didn't, but that didn't mean that much. I hear they sit in the stores and when they see someone not pays, they come out and put a ticket on the cars. I took another glance to the right, to the left, and to the right and to the left across the street. I jogged across the street. To a smoke shop and grabbed a wrap and something to drink. I got the change, I didn't even feel like coming down here. But, I had an impromptu meeting that I didn't want to flake on. I came back to the car after getting change for the meter and sat in the car and rolled up. Then got out and wrapped my lips around the blunt and headed to the meter machine to get a ticket from the machine to get a meter ticket to put on the car. I was wrapping the end of the blunt and was in my pocket getting another dollar out.

I heard. "Didn't you just get out of trouble?"
I looked offended quizzically around to find the voice.

"I just sat and watched you roll that."

I really didn't know what to say, so I searched for a smile, but my heart was sunken in from the interaction.

"Hey."

"Hi."

I placed the blunt in the pouch of my hoodie and tried to concentrate on getting the parking ticket out of the machine. I really didn't have much to say, nor could I find a conversation to participate in at the moment.

"Can I get a hug?"

I turned to give a hug as the ticket printed out. And figured out to say a.

"How are you?"

"I'm good."

"That's good."

"Um I have to put this on this on the car."

"Go ahead."

I walked to the car and she stood there. I really didn't want to come back to the conversation but I walked back. I pulled out the phone to see what time it was, I had about 15 minutes.

"You need to go?"

"Well you cutting into my smoke time, but I got about ten minutes."

"How are you?"

"I'm good."

"Are we good?"

"Yeah, we good. How could I not be, nothing ever transpired between us, I mean I was caught in some feelings, that shouldn't have been there any ways. And sent some energy your way that I definitely sent your way and needed to re-protect and retract."

"I'm around for the rest of the night, are you busy?"

"Actually, after I finished with this meeting, I was actually pretty much done for the night."

"Well after this meeting, my evening is pretty open."

"Ok, so a date then?"

"A date?"

"Yes, a date."

"A date?"

"Yes, a date?"

"Ok, I said hesitantly."

"Put your number in my phone, so I can text you where I'm at and so you can have some smoke time."

"I think my high was blown, before I even was faded."

I took her phone from her hand and put my number in and handed it back to her, a piece of me hope it didn't save. But she pushed sent and you heard my phone ring from the car.

"I hear it."

"You're leaving your phone in the car?"

To be honest, I wasn't, but it didn't matter much.

"I'll text you in a few."

"Ok, well my phone is in the car. I'll see it when I get out of my meeting."

"Get your phone out of the car."

"I have my other phone in my pocket, I'm good. That's my personal number."

I didn't mean to be coming off weird, but I definitely was still in my feelings about how nothing transpired between us.

She gave me another hug and I hugged her. She let out a "mmm" sound. She kissed my neck.

"Are you going to your car?"

"No, I'm in here." she turned and pointed to the store.

"Ok, I was just going to walk you to your car."

"Ok, thank you. I still am waiting for them to polish some things. Just make sure when I text you, you respond."

"Ok, yeah, I will. Let me be on my way."

"Ok."

I walked to the corner and made my turn so I could light my el. I had so many thoughts in my head and none of them were the ones I wanted to be in my head. First of all, a date? Like a date date, I was stressing about what to wear. She's always been somewhat out of my league socially, like not really, but on sight, I'm a regular type of individual and she definitely the type that was on the scene. Thing was, we knew some of the same people, but I had actually gone back in to my shell, and just was working on wealth. I am not the type that needs to be seen really. Although, I like nice toys, which makes me stand out. I guess, I had to go take the car to get detailed. The thought of impressing her and not impressing her went through the mind. I lit the dutch and just tried to not think about it until my meeting was over. I walked around the block and tried to take the eight minutes I had until my meeting, letting my mind breath and relax because it was definitely pinned up and jammed. I stopped and looked in the tattoo shop and then headed to my meeting. Grabbed the oil out of my pocket and rubbed it all over my neck and wrists. I walked three minutes to the meeting.

I double checked the address in my phone and then rang the doorbell, I was buzzed in rather quickly. There was a voice on the intercom.

"Hey, I'm on the second floor."

I started up the stairs. A door opened.

"Hey, in here."

I'd became comfortable with just doing business with people oppose to having a team. No, you can't do it by yourself, but I've found just hiring people and doing business with people was better than trying to get people to be on the same page as you.

Someone said loosely quoted.

"You're a fool for expecting someone to believe in your vision the way that you do." Although, I didn't necessarily want others to believe in my vision, I just wanted to connect visions. But understanding that as a concept help some things move in the right direction. We sat and had our meeting for about an hour. Very productive meeting. We wrapped it up and said we would meet again next month around the same time, and that I should expect to see some changes, and just save my question for our next meeting unless it was dire important. I was glad that I had put enough in the meter for an hour and a half. I had about fifteen minutes left until the meter expired. I walked around the block to the car. I kinda hoped she was finished or at least didn't see me going to the car. I didn't really look to see if she was around, I actually just tried to slide in the car without being seen, I tried to pull out the spot quick and smooth. I pulled out the spot and headed to go grab something to eat. Five minutes in to my drive I heard the phone that I left in the car buzz. I opened up the arm rest and took the phone out at the light.

"Address."

I texted back.

"What were you trying to do tonight?"

"You tell me, you are taking me on a date."

"Do you want to get something to eat? Or do you want to do something."

"It doesn't matter."

"Ok, I'll see if I can make reservations somewhere, and if I can, we can grab something to eat."

"Ok. That sounds good."

"Ok."

I don't really make reservations or really go out often, I prefer to cook to be honest with you. And, actually thought perhaps, I could find a kitchen we could make a meal. I looked up and did a search for a kitchen like that, I couldn't find one, so I just made reservations. I made them for seven o'clock.

I really didn't have anything to wear, I actually headed to get something to wear. I am usually in athletic or casual wear. And since I had to get rid of my clothes, due to an infestation years back, I never really re invested in my wardrobe just yet. I wasn't sure of my style at this time in my life.

I headed to the store and had to find another parking spot. It took me about an hour, but I grabbed something to wear. I headed back to my place.

I texted. "Hey, reservations at seven."

No reply. I thought perhaps this was all a joke and she was going to stand me up. I started worrying, thought had I wasted my time making reservations? Had I wasted my time getting something to wear. I got back to my spot and then I made a call. The phone rang three times, before there was a

"Hello." on the other end.

"Hello. I was. Just letting you know that the reservations were at 7."

"Ok, thank you for calling and letting me know. What time should I be ready."

"Six fifteen is fine."

"Ok. Again, thank you for calling and letting me know."

"Sure."

"I'd gotten a bit worried, thought you…"

"Thought, I was what?"

"Nothing."

"I should be there around six fifteen."

It was two thirty or so now and at the top of the day I thought I was going to have just another lounge around day. Here I am getting ready for a date. I called my hair braider to see if I could get some braids right quick and thankfully she was available. I told her that I would be taking a nap and then would be over. Around five o'clock. She doesn't take long, so I figure five to five thirty, get my hair braided and be on my way by six o'clock. Since my measurements were wrong. I called her back the phone rang.

She answered with a, "Yes?"

"Hey, I know I said six fifteen, but more like six thirty, I have to get my hair braided."

"Ok, thank you for letting me know."

"Ok."

"Ok, see you soon."

"Yes, see you soon."

...to be continued.

I Like How You Like Me

Grabbing some sleep, we had a ladies night at the club. I thought it was one of the dancers or my business partner. I didn't really look at the phone.

Raspy voice. "Hey."

"Hi."

"Hi."

I recognized the voice but wished I missed the call.

"Hi."

"Hi."

Hi went on for about minute.

"What's up with you?"

I guess I was heartbroken but didn't really have a right to be.

"I'm grabbing a nap."

"Oh, you were sleep? But it's two pm."

My line clicked in.

"Can you hold on, my line has an incoming call."

"Hey."

"Hey."

It was one of the dancers.

"You got room for me?"

"Sure I'll put you on the list."

"Ok babe, thanks."

I went back to the other line.

"Hello?"

I kinda wished she'd hung up but she was still on the line.

"Hey."

"Hi."

"What's up with you?"

"Nothing, you don't feel like talking?"

"I mean, I don't think we have anything to really talk about, do we?"

"Is that how you feel?"

"Is it something you needed?"

"I needed to see you."

"Why you needed to see me for?"

"I can't come see you?"

"I got somethings to do tonight."

"What are you doing now?"

"Well I was getting some sleep for what I needed to do tonight."

"So, you don't want to see me?"

"If you want to come through you can."

"Okay, I'm coming through."

I gave her the code to get in.

"You not going to come down?"

"Call me when you get here."

"Okay."

I hung up the phone and tried to gather myself. I really was very interested in her, but it didn't seem

like she was interested in me the way I wanted her to be interested. And maybe it was for the best.

feel back into a light sleep. About twenty minutes later my phone rang, I didn't know she was coming so soon.

"Hello?"

As I picked up the phone.

"I'm five minutes away."

"Okay."

I peeled myself out of the bed and put my slides on my feet. I headed down to the parking spots and sat on the steps. She pulled up shortly. I got up, as she parked and headed to her car. She got out the the car after parking. The sun was still out it was pretty nice a cool breeze and the shade of the trees provided an extra breeze.

"There's a dish in the back seat."

She looked cute as usual, she had on a cute dress. It's lasagna.

"It's still hot, so be careful."

She knew that was my favorite meal.

"Thank you."

"You're welcome."

"Is there anything else?"

"No, that's it."

I closed the door and waited for her to grab her purse. We walked to the door of the building. I opened the door.

Told her to enter her pin, she entered her pin in the keypad. That was installed, the door unlocked, we entered the door way and we headed to the kitchen to put the food on the counter.

"Watch your hands."

I placed the dish on the counter and went to get a plate.

"What's wrong with you?"

I never understood why females wanted to act like you aren't suppose to be hurt or you are suppose to give them the same treatment when they aren't your girl.

"Nothing, what's up? Are you eating?"

"I don't know, am I eating off of your plate?"

"It's up to you."

I replied.

"Well since you being a tad weird, I'll take a plate."

I continued to pile extra on the plate. I walked to the silverware drawer and got two forks. I walked to the table, I grabbed some pomegranate juices from the refrigerator and sat down.

"Thank you, for making me something to eat."

"You're welcome."

"What's up with you, why the cold shoulder?"

"There's no cold shoulder, how do you want me to be? You fuck with some one right?"

"I mean, it's not like that."

I prayed over the food and took a fork full.

"It's none of my business really as long as you're happy and not in harms way, it's good."

"Is that how you feel?"

"Pretty much."

"I don't think you should feel that way."

"I don't know if you can control feelings, but that's how I feel. Am I suppose to feel differently?"

I'm not certain as to why I asked that because I really didn't want to get in such a conversation. It was my emotions that responded so quickly. My phone rang, it was closer to her, she picked it up and accepted the call.

"Hello? Who's this?"

The person must've responded because as I shook my head in shock she handed me the phone without saying anything.

"Peace?"

As I answered the phone.

"Sure, there's room in the lineup. Ok, no problem. No, I'm good, thanks for asking. ok, yelp, ten to fifteen minutes depending on who shows up. Ok, love, see you later."
I ended the phone call and put the phone on the chair.

"So, who was that?"

I looked at her, with a you're really concerned expression and answered hesitantly.

"It was an entertainer for tonight."

"Oh, ok."

She really didn't know what I did and I left it vague, because I don't like personal situations to be swayed by what I do in the entertainment sector.

"Oh, ok." she replied.

I guess she didn't have much to say because the conversation matched the response. I went back to my plate or our plate. She took a fork full and asked me to open her juice. I'd forgot the paper towels so after I opened it, I got up to get the napkins.

"Where are you going?" She said.

"Getting paper towels and the remote from the other table."
And sat down.

"You, you're really acting shitty."

"What do you want me to be like?"

"It doesn't matter, you haven't asked me how I was, or nothing."

"How are you?"

She stared at me like I was being condescending, but I wasn't.

"B, how do you want me to be?"

"You didn't even hug me. I've missed you. Do you miss me?

Why should I miss you, if you wanted to be here, you would be and you know that B."

"Well, I've missed you."

"'Cause you wanted to miss me, it's nothing personal. Just, I don't do situations well, either a bitch fucks with me or not and you don't really and that's cool."

"Look, I missed you and I cooked for you, so don't say I don't fuck with you."

I was so shut down emotionally on this topic. My phone rang again, she picked it up before I could reach for it, she hit declined.

"Babe, please don't answer the phone right now, while we are talking."

She handed it to me, it was another dancer. I hit declined and texted back.

"So, you're going to text. B, I have to respond, I actually have something to do in a couple of hours. So, on the low, I'm slightly busy, I'm sorry.

She took the phone from my hand and came and straddled me.

"I've missed you."

She slid her hands in my shorts, she took her other hand and picked my arm up to put it around her waist. She started kissing me. I had missed her too, but I didn't at all want to show it, but I know she could feel it. She touched my clit and smiled and chuckled.

"Well, I don't know if you've missed me, but you definitely still like me."

She squeezed my breast and dropped down to her knees then pulled my shorts down and put me in her mouth. She sucked me like her favorite piece of candy. She felt so good, her mouth was so warm and wet, she savored me like a favorite dish.

"Am I doing it right?"

I let out a breathy, "yes."

Nothings like a feminine woman sucking me off and enjoy doing it."

"Are you going to come for me?"

I barley could respond with a "huh"?

My voice cracked the entire time trying to get the word out, "fuck."

Pushed her mouth off of me and brought her up to me. I tilted my head back and placed her in my mouth.

"I want you inside of me so bad."

I put my fingers inside of her while she guided my hands inside of her.

"Baby, I want you inside of me."

She said riding my fingers.

"Can we go to the bedroom?" she requested.

We have never been that intimate, that way. She kissed me and took my fingers out of her and took my hand. I held her hand as we walked to the microwave together. I put the rest of the food in there. I squeezed her hand, led her to the bedroom. I excused my self she asked.

"Where are you going?

I responded with a, "huh?"

Found it to be an embarrassing question.

"No, do that here."

I opened the drawer.

"Can I help you put it on you?"

Although, it was turning me on, it was a bit embarrassing.

"You trying to put all of that inside of me?"

"Huh?"

"You heard me."

"I mean, yeah, am I too much? I'll be gentle I promise."

As she tightened the left harness strap and grabbed the extended me and stroked me.

"You sure, you want me?"

"Yes."

I sat next to her on the bed as she stroked me. They say we aren't suppose to feel being touched, but I felt her stroking the extended me. It aroused me even more, I told her to come here, so I could remove the dress she had on. I sat down on the bed and crawled body length to the head board, she climbed up after me and laid down I turned to her and positioned myself over her. She looked at me and open her legs I took her hand and placed it on my strap and told her put me inside. She placed the tip inside as we pushed me inside of her slowly. She let out a "mmmm" as I pushed in deep inside her, she exhaled a "yes." I started to look for the rhythm, she responded with "yes." She felt so good, she wasn't really a breast person, but hers were so pretty, my mouth hungered for them. I put her back in my mouth to feel them respond.

Acknowledgements

I appreciate any crush that I wasn't brave enough to approach.

Glossary

In this book there are some profanity words. I have edited words at times to cut down on the actual use of curse words.

Shii =Shit

Niguh = N word but in a friendly form

Nahwl = No

Knahwl = No

Aiyte = Alright

Bitchin' = complaining

Fuk'n/ Fuk/ Fuch = The F word

MF = MotherF word-er

Buhl = Guy

Fiya = Good or great

Shawtie = Term of endearment for a female you are getting to know

Finnuh/Fittin = About to

Ma = Term of endearment for a female.

Smedium = A smalle medium size that fits too small or very snug.

Dem = Them

Spanish Words are Spanish Words (used as best as I knew how)

French Words are French Words (used as best as I knew how)

Thanks for
Reading

K.K.T,
Raggdoll
Publishing

Made in the USA
Middletown, DE
28 October 2024